Suspended in a nightmare

"Quick, shut the door!" Kristen shouted. *"Shut the door!"*

We slammed the door hard on the creature, but were unable to close it completely. The werewolf snarled in pain and struck the wood with all his force. The door cracked open. A glistening black snout edged around the panel, pinkish tongue licking its lips. Demon-red eyes appeared and zeroed in on my terrified face. A hairy paw raked through the air, missing my hands by inches.

The werewolf threw back its head and howled, in hungry anticipation.

"Put more weight against the door!" Kristen cried.

I did as she commanded, but it wasn't working.

The force and power of the werewolf pushed the door open inch by terrifying inch. Another few inches and it would shove its way into the kitchen.

Kristen and I couldn't hold on. She was stronger than me, but we were both getting tired.

"What are we going to do?" I shouted.

The werewolf was snarling, enraged, slamming its weight against the flimsy barricade.

The repeated force of its blows made Kristen and me slide across the linoleum in our slippers. One more foot. . . . Six more inches . . .

The beast was so close I could feel its hot breath on my face.

A yellowed fang nipped close to my fingers.

Fiendly Corners #3

REVENGE OF THE HAIRY HORROR

By E. W. Leroe

Hyperion Paperbacks for Children
New York

First Hyperion Paperback edition 1996

Printed in the United States of America.

1 3 5 7 9 10 8 6 4 2

The text for this book is set in 11-point Palatino.

Designed by Joann Hill-Lovinski.

Library of Congress Cataloging-in-Publication Data
Leroe, Ellen, (date)
Revenge of the Hairy Horror / E.W. Leroe. — 1st Hyperion
Paperback ed.
p.   cm. — (Fiendly Corners; 3)
Summary: Matt and his bratty cousin Kristen are spooked when the monster
in an old werewolf movie comes to life and menaces their town.
ISBN 0-7868-1097-1 (pbk.)
[1. Werewolves—Fiction.   2. Horror stories.]   I. Title.
II. Series: Leroe, Ellen, 1949–   Fiendly Corners ; 3.
PZ7.L5614Re   1996
[Fic]—dc20   96-4318

For Susan (Soni) Goodman, good friend, talented writer, and invaluable brainstormer!
—E. W. L.

CHAPTER ONE

The last thing I expected to see in my bedroom was a werewolf.

Baring its fangs, it growled at me and prepared to pounce. I stared at the ratty sneakers on its feet, the over-sized rubber snout sliding off its nose, the scruffy fur that didn't quite cover its paws, and rolled my eyes in disgust.

"You think that costume's going to get you into the matinee today?" I said.

My best friend, Sean O' Shea, who looked more like a skinny red-haired rodent than a terrifying wolf man, peeled off his mask with a scowl.

"Give me a break, Matt," he whined. "This was the last thing I could find in the costume rack at Magic Vision. I know it's too big, but the smaller-sized werewolf outfits were gone."

I pulled Sean over to the full-length mirror on my bedroom closet and made him look at the both of us.

"You want authentic werewolf?" I said. With one dramatic movement, I dropped down on all fours and threw back my head and howled. "This will beat your tatty costume any day. And I don't even need a moth-ridden fur suit."

Sean watched me get up with that doom-and-gloom expression he always wears.

"I'm not going to get in free at the matinee today, am

I?" he said. "I knew this costume was awful, but I kept hoping I could pull it off." He fumbled around in his costume and pulled out a clipping. "At least that's what my horoscope said for today: 'You will battle great odds and achieve the impossible.' "

"Oh, brother," I muttered.

Sean is a really good friend of mine. (My best friend, and my only friend, I hate to admit.) Because he lives right across the street from me, we see each other all the time. But his belief in horoscopes, superstitions, and good luck charms drives me crazy. I stared at our reflection in the mirror and grinned. Talk about a strange-looking duo.

Sean is tall and skinny, with a mop of reddish hair, a face full of freckles, and the look of having slept in a clothes dryer. Sean's the most messy, mismatched person you'd ever hope to see. Nothing ever fits on Sean. Even his werewolf costume was bagging at the knees and hanging off his long arms. I, on the other hand, am short, dark, and chubby, just like everyone else in the Walstrom family. "Moon-faced," some kids at school tease me. The class jerk, Todd Slivack, calls me Matt the Fat, or Fatty Matty. At least I'm neat, though. The original Organization Man. I make lists of everything I need to do, I alphabetize my schoolbooks in the shelves, I color code my clothes in the closet. I can't help it. I'm a neatnik.

Slobby Sean and I are complete opposites.

Yet we have one thing in common. We love classic horror movies, especially the ones made in the '40s, '50s and early '60s. We're into *Dracula, Frankenstein, The Phantom of the Opera,* and *Doctor Jekyll and Mr. Hyde.* Kids in our seventh-grade class at Friendly Corners Middle School call us the Monster Twins because we talk about scary films all the time. And luckily for us, the one movie theater in the town of Friendly Corners, the Palace, plays scary flicks nonstop. The owner, Calvin Coughin—"Coffin's my name," he always states, "horror's my game"—is into spooky stuff as much as we are and calls himself Commander Coffin. There's a club a lot of kids belong to—the Coffin Club, where you get discount tickets to matinees, special prices on popcorn and soda, and are eligible to win free passes to shows if you come wearing crazy costumes or outfits.

That's why Sean and I were playing at being werewolves on this cold and wintery Tuesday afternoon of Thanksgiving week. The Palace was (topping off its werewolf month) with a double feature at 2 P.M.: *Frankenstein Meets the Wolf Man* with Bela Lugosi and *I Was a Teenage Werewolf* with Michael Landon. Commander Coffin had promised free tickets to kids showing up in the best werewolf outfits. I didn't want to wear a costume, but I was hoping my two "knock knock" jokes would persuade Commander Coffin to let me in free.

I tapped on Sean's head. "Knock knock!"

"Hey," he grumbled, rubbing his forehead. "Take it easy."

I made to knock against his head again, when he hastily said, "Who's there?"

"Howl," I replied.

"Howl who?"

"Howl I ever tell my parents I'm a wolf man?" I said, and promptly burst into snickers.

Sean stared blankly at me. "Ha-ha."

"You don't like that one," I said. "I've got another." I tapped my friend's head and said, "Knock knock."

Sean rolled his eyes but said, "Who's there?"

"Ow!"

"Ow who?"

I bared imaginary fangs at him. "So you're a were-wolf, too!"

Sean laughed, then his face crumpled. "You're going to get a free pass and I'm going to have to pay," he said in a gloomy voice. He kicked at the wolf man mask on the floor. "I always lose."

I sighed and picked up the mask. "How many times do I have to tell you? Think positively."

"Yeah," he said. "I'm *positively* stupid-looking in this getup and I'm *positively* not going to get in free."

I shook my head (that's Sean for you), when the door burst open. A tiny figure in a purple-and-green-striped T-shirt and baggy jeans jumped into the room, punching and kicking in wild karate moves. Following on his heels was our big yellow Lab retriever, Puddles.

"Hey, Rat-Face!" I angrily shouted. "You're not invited in here!" I glared at Puddles, who wagged his tail and jumped up on me. "And you're not, either."

My karate-kicking seven-year-old brother, Chase, immediately leapt onto my bed and began jumping up and down on it as if it were a trampoline.

"I know a secret," he said in that singsong voice I hated. "I know a secret!" he repeated.

I stared at my brother who was grinning at me and Sean. Unfortunately, Chase takes after the family, so he looks like a miniature version of me. He has dark thick hair, chocolate brown eyes, chubby cheeks, and the same roly-poly body. Unlike me, he's obnoxious, loud, constantly follows you around, and tells silly jokes.

"What's the secret?" Sean asked.

Chase stopped jumping on my bed long enough to motion Sean over.

"Don't do it," I warned Sean. "He's just showing off."

"I am not," Chase shouted. "I'll tell Sean and not you."

Sean can't pass up reading a horoscope or hearing a secret, so he walked over to the bed. My brother leaned down close to him, cupped a hand over Sean's ear, and suddenly screamed, "Yaaaaa!"

"Hey!" Sean yelled, jumping straight up in the air. "You little jerk!"

"Get out, right now," I ordered Chase.

"I know a secret, I know a secret," Chase shouted, and jumped off the bed as I lunged toward him. "Aunt Helen and Uncle Darryl's here and guess who's with them?"

I stopped dead. A small uneasy knot formed in my stomach.

"Not the B Girl," I muttered in horrified disbelief. "She wasn't supposed to be here until Thanksgiving!"

"Well, she's here!" Chase shouted happily. "And she's got a big suitcase, so she must be staying."

I sank on the bed, my heart hammering.

"Who's the B Girl?" Sean said.

"Kristen Powers, my stuck-up older cousin," I explained. "I call her B for *b*ossy, *b*ragging, thinks-she's-*b*etter-than-anyone-else *b*umblebee. She was here two years ago before my aunt and uncle moved to Los Angeles and she nearly drove me crazy, daring me to do all this crazy stuff. I can't believe she's going to be staying with us."

"Yeah, I remember her now," Sean said, snapping his fingers. "A tiny little thing with short fuzzy yellow hair and great big eyes. She was kind of quiet and shy, I thought."

I jumped up with a scowl. "You don't know Kristen at

11

all. She's about as quiet and shy as Godzilla. And why she's invading our house just when we're on vacation is beyond me. She's going to ruin everything. You wait and see."

As if in sympathy, Puddles padded over and licked my hands and arms. Suddenly, he turned to face the bedroom window and began barking.

"What's with him?" Sean asked. "He's acting like an attack dog."

"Cut it out," I shouted at Puddles, but my crazy dog kept growling ferociously and barking. He scratched at the windowsill.

Two seconds later we heard a knocking sound against the side of the house and Puddles jumped at the closed window.

"Stupid mutt," I said. I bent over, trying to restrain him.

Behind me Chase let out a high-pitched squeal and pointed to the window. Sean yelped and bumped against the bed.

"What is going on?" I muttered and turned to look out the window.

A face in a dark cap popped up against the glass, large and frightening, dark eyes staring in at us. A fist pounded on the window.

I stumbled against my own feet and let out a horrified scream.

CHAPTER TWO

"Hey, it's me," the frightening figure shouted. "It's Kristen, for pity's sake."

"Kristen?" I mumbled, still in a dazed shock.

"Open this window before I fall out of the tree!"

I edged closer to the window, peering out at the blurry face. At my feet Puddles was going crazy, teeth bared, growling. Now that I had a better view, I could see my cousin clinging to the top branch of the old maple tree just outside my bedroom window. (The tree that we were expressly instructed never to climb.) Kristen was wearing a camouflage-type baseball cap on her head, an olive green army jacket, and funny black boots. She looked like an escapee from some commando movie.

I was happy to note that her stuck-up little nose was pink from the cold.

"Hey, come on!" she yelled, pounding at the glass. "Get me in here before I freeze to death!"

What a great idea, I thought, pretending to scratch my head and give it some consideration. Just leave the B Girl outside until she turned into a frozen Popsicle, then cracked off under the weight of a squirrel.

"Matthew," Kristen said in that warning tone of hers. The same tone she used before she'd sneak up behind me and tickle my sides and armpits. She'd get me laughing so hard I'd snort like a wounded elephant, and then

13

everyone would laugh at me. I may have been laughing, but inside I hated it. I hated her.

There were footsteps coming up the stairs.

"What in the world is going on up here?" my mom demanded, popping up in the doorway. Right behind her was my aunt Helen. The women were sisters, but they looked—and acted—completely different. My mom was dark-haired, plump, and loved to stay at home. She and my dad ran a bridal consulting business, the Bridal Path, right out of our house. My aunt Helen, on the other hand, was tall, blond, and practically lived out of a suitcase because she and my uncle Darryl traveled so much. She and my uncle are known professionally as the Amazing Powers, two daredevils who fly stunt planes at air shows. Not only that, but my aunt and uncle are into rock climbing, surfing, and bungee-jumping, anything to do with thrills and danger. Kristen must have inherited the excitement gene from her parents, because she was always bragging about her skateboarding, karate, and triathlon competitions. Personally I never believed a word of it, but seeing her perched on that tree two stories up made me wonder.

Now I pointed at the window and Kristen's pinched-looking face.

I couldn't wait for the expected explosion.

It didn't come. My mom gave a worried cry and hurried to slide the window open. When Kristen tumbled in, my aunt Helen clapped her on the back with an approving grin.

"That's my girl," she exclaimed proudly. "Always getting into scrapes."

Scrapes? My mouth dropped open. Was I hearing correctly? Aunt Helen was actually praising Kristen for

14

climbing up a tree and scaring us half to death? And was I seeing correctly, as well? The tiny little bumblebee from two years before had shot up nearly four inches and was as tall as Aunt Helen. Not only that but Kristen seemed to have muscle and curves hiding behind the army fatigues.

My mom hugged Kristen, but gave her a little shake.

"If you're going to be staying with us while your parents are performing at an air show, then you're going to have to follow our rules. And the Walstrom family forbids tree climbing, understand?"

"Sure, Aunt Val," Kristen said. She gave my mom a phony I'm-sorry smile, then shot a gloating grin my way.

My mom nudged me forward. "Matt, what's wrong with you? Say hello to Kristen and Aunt Helen properly. You haven't seen them in over two years."

I readily hugged Aunt Helen, but stopped short of embracing Kristen. She had that I'm-going-to-tickle-you-if-you-take-a-step-closer gleam in her eyes.

"Hey, Dristan, I mean, Kristen," I said in a dull voice. I nodded over at Sean, who was standing up straight for a change and staring at my cousin with a peculiar gleam in his own eyes.

"This is Sean O' Shea," I said. "You met him briefly when you visited us at Christmas some years ago, but you probably don't remember."

"I remember," Kristen said, smiling at Sean.

Sean actually blushed and shuffled his feet.

Suddenly Kristen whipped off her cap. A mass of waist-length blond hair tumbled over her shoulders and slid over dive-bomber green eyes. Eyes that stared directly into yours without blinking.

"It's going to be great staying with you for the Thanksgiving holidays," she said. "And celebrating my

15

thirteenth birthday with my favorite aunt and uncle. And favorite cousins," she hastily added.

I inwardly groaned. I had forgotten that the B Girl's birthday fell on Thanksgiving and now we had to celebrate the day with her. Why couldn't Aunt Helen or Uncle Darryl spend the day with us? As if echoing my thoughts, Aunt Helen hugged Kristen and gave us a guilty smile.

"Darryl and I hated to leave our baby on her birthday, but we had a last minute air show to do. But I know staying the week with you will more than make up for our not being here."

Mom shot me a be-nice look. "Matthew and Chase will be delighted to make Kristen's birthday a special day. In fact, in our family, we allow the birthday person a special week and grant his or her every wish. Won't that be fun to do for Kristen, boys?"

"Yaaaaa!" Chase shouted happily, and grabbed onto Kristen's hands.

I nodded unenthusiastically. Just what I needed, I thought. Celebrating Miss Bossy's birthday on Thanksgiving. At least it made sense, however. A turkey born on Turkey Day. Before I could stop it, my lips curled. Seeing me trying to disguise a smile, Kristen edged in closer and squeezed my sides.

"Something funny, Matt-ee-ee-ee?" she said, tickling my sides and armpits with each "ee."

I wriggled in her grasp, but couldn't get away.

I'm not going to laugh, I told myself. I'm not going to laugh. . . . I burst out laughing, embarrassing snorts that sounded like a hiccuping rhino.

Everyone cracked up, including my (former) best friend.

Even Puddles, my (new) best friend, jumped up and slobbered over Kristen. He licked her face and hands. Chase jumped up and down in front of her and whispered, "I've got a secret! I've got a secret!"

Kristen stopped tickling me and turned to him. "Really? Want to hear my secret first?"

My brother nodded, eyes solemn and large. She motioned him closer and bent down until she was leaning right up against his ear. Taking a deep breath, she opened her mouth and screamed, "Yaaaaaa!"

Little Space Case is going to lose it now, I thought, mentally rubbing my hands together.

But my brother shot in the air, yelped loudly, then fell on the floor laughing.

Kristen couldn't lose, I realized. Miss Queen Bee makes another conquest. Couldn't my family, friend, and dog see through her?

The front door slammed and we heard footsteps below.

"Where in the world is everybody?" my uncle Darryl boomed from the bottom of the stairs. "I need help in bringing all of Kris's things inside."

I stared at my cousin.

"Things?" I said suspiciously. "What things?"

She gave an airy wave. "Oh, just sports stuff. My skateboard, my bike, my kick bag . . . ."

"Kick bag?" Sean piped up. "This I gotta see."

"It's for my karate workouts," Kristen said. "I'm working on getting my brown belt."

"Cool," Sean said.

"You can teach me!" Chase cried, pulling at my cousin's hand.

We rushed downstairs, greeting Uncle Darryl.

Kristen, Sean, and Chase ran outside to the Powers's van, while I stayed in the hall, examining the suitcases and bags lined up beside the front door. Kristen hadn't exaggerated. She really did have *stuff*. In addition to the hand weights and ankle weights stuffed inside a canvas bag, she had brought along a box of books, a sack full of junk food, and the collection of teddy bears that I remembered from her last visit. Strange as it seemed, my tough-as-nails cousin loved teddy bears as much as I loved horror movies.

Finally all her assorted equipment and clothes were sitting in the inside hall. Uncle Darryl and Aunt Helen plopped wearily on chairs in the living room, and my mom went to make coffee. While Kristen was showing off the latest moves in karate to Sean and Chase, I snuck a peek at my watch. Twenty minutes to two. Sean and I had to hustle if we wanted to get to the Palace for the contest. We lived a short distance to town, on a shady, tree-lined street four blocks away. If we left now, we'd get there in plenty of time.

"Uh, Mom," I said, trying to get her attention as she returned with the coffee and cookies. "Sean and I have to get going if we're going to make the matinee."

"What matinee?" Kristen said, wheeling around.

"Oh, it's nothing," I began, but Sean interrupted me. He babbled all about the Palace theater and Commander Coffin's scary movie matinees. "And today they're beginning a month devoted to werewolves by showing two great classics."

Please don't say you want to go, I silently prayed. Please don't say—

"I want to go," Kristen said.

"I want to go, too," Chase announced. He was staring

up at my cousin with undisguised admiration in his eyes. Now that I noticed it, so was Sean.

"You can't go," my mom said, "you're spending the afternoon with Jason."

Chase's bottom lip quivered.

"But, Kristen," my mom continued, "Matt would love to have you join him. Right, Matt?"

My heart sank. What could I say with Aunt Helen and Uncle Darryl peering happily into my face?

"Fine," I muttered. "Let me grab my jacket and money."

Not only was my most hated bossy cousin staying with our family for the Thanksgiving holiday, but now she was crossing the line into my territory.

"Remember," my mom said to me as the three of us left the house, "it's Kristen's birthday week, so whatever she says, goes."

"Ducky," I muttered with a dark scowl, and slammed the front door.

CHAPTER THREE

Kristen turned into a whirling tornado the minute we left the house.

Ever the show-off, she kicked at trees, jumped off curbs, and sprinted a good distance in front of us, then circled back to laugh at our slow pace.

"You guys are snails," she said. "You're slugs. I dare you to race me down the street, and I'll even run backwards to make it harder."

"I can beat you," Sean said.

He'd look like an idiot, pounding down the street in a baggy werewolf outfit, but Sean was too smitten with Queen Bee to realize that fact.

"In your dreams," Kristen retorted. She crouched low, then spun around, whipping her leg out to connect with my head. She missed by inches.

"Hey!" I shouted, clutching at my chest in fright. Heart thudding rapidly, I glared at Kristen who gave me the wide-eyed, innocent look.

"I wasn't going to hurt you, Matt," she said. "I was just goofing around."

"Yeah, right," I muttered. "You almost gave me a heart attack."

She tossed her cap in the air, then caught it in her teeth. (What a show-off.) "You need something to wake you up. This town is dead enough as it is."

"It is not," I retorted. "It's got a lot more going for it than L.A."

My cousin looked around the countryside with a sarcastic smile.

"I don't think so," she said. We were walking along the weather-beaten arched bridge that crossed the river. The small shopping district of Friendly Corners was just beyond the bridge. "This town is smaller than the parking lot of my high school back home. And judging by the people and fields and cows I've seen, a whole lot sleepier."

I trudged along behind Kristen and Sean, glowering at her long blond hair. Sure, it was one thing for my friends and me to poke fun at Friendly Corners, a picturesque small town with woods, a winding river, and an old-fashioned town square with a park and little shops. But I had lived here all my life and I *liked* it here.

Besides, small and boring as it seemed, the town possessed a secret.

An eerie, mysterious secret that only the kids at the middle school knew about.

Friendly Corners was haunted.

Watching Kristen playfully punch Sean's arm and joke around with him made me wish a spirit would spring up in front of my cousin at this very moment and scare her to death.

"Awesome," I heard Sean compliment Kristen as she jumped onto the bridge railing (crazy show-off!) and took a few high-wire steps. She dropped down gracefully onto the walkway without ruffling a hair. "Now I dare you," she said to me. "I dare you to do that."

I shook my head, annoyed to be shown up in front of my best friend. When the time was right, I'd dare her to something she'd have to refuse. Until then, however, why

21

not let her in on the town's scary secret and see if I could ruffle her fearless image?

"I wasn't going to mention this, but I think I should," I said. "Since you're going to be spending some time in Friendly Corners." I lowered my voice and dramatically peered over my shoulder before I continued. "Friendly Corners *is* dead, you were right, but not in the way you think. Friendly Corners is haunted."

Kristen stopped so abruptly she bumped straight into Sean. Sean immediately blushed and began babbling apologies. But my cousin wasn't listening to Sean. She was gazing at me with an intense expression in those cat-like green eyes. And for once, she wasn't smirking. Had I gotten through to the Fearless Wonder, after all?

"What are you talking about?" she said. She gazed at me, then turned to look at Sean. "He's being stupid, isn't he? Making a joke about the town being haunted?"

Sean swallowed, afraid to say something that might bother Kristen, yet unable to lie.

"Well, it's true. At least, a lot of kids say it's true," he hastened to add. "Matt and I have never seen anything spooky happen, but Tyler Harrison and Bryan Hartley, classmates of ours, swear they've heard voices and seen *things*."

Kristen made a face. "What kind of things?"

Time for me to get into the act. I pointed up ahead to the entrance to town.

"See that big 'Welcome to Friendly Corners' sign that crosses Main Street?" I narrowed my eyes, let my voice go soft and creepy. "Sometimes the reflectorized letter in the word Friendly blinks off, as if an invisible monster's fist is covering it. Then the name of the town changes into *Fiendly* Corners. And when it does, an evil thick mist slides in from across the river and blankets the entire shopping area. Things come alive in the night," I added, remembering things I had heard. "Faces appear in the old-fashioned lampposts in the town square. Bony chilled hands reach out from behind trees."

"This is ridiculous," Kristen sputtered, shaking her head. Yet her voice didn't sound all that brave and convincing. She was staring down the end of the pedestrian lane of the bridge, as if expecting to see a misty form surround the welcome sign and block out the letter *R*.

"You're just making all this stupid stuff up to get back at me for scaring you in the bedroom," Kristen insisted.

I shrugged and didn't answer her. I exchanged meaningful glances with Sean.

Kristen tossed her long hair angrily and scowled.

"Come on, you guys, be real. *Why* would a town the size of a postage stamp be haunted?"

"The Singing Stones," I said in a whisper. "The Singing Stones haunt Friendly Corners."

As if on cue, Sean and I nodded. We both began edging along the walkway, forcing an obviously reluctant Kristen to move closer to town. Her feet dragged. She began to fiddle with her hair.

"What's Singing Stones?" she asked in a small voice.

"I'll tell you about the Stones," Sean offered. His eyes lit up. As much as he liked Kristen, and I could tell he was bonkers, Sean liked ghost stories more. Now he lowered his voice as he marched along. "Singing Stones is up on the Ridge, above town, deep in the woods. It's the site of a meteorite crash that happened years ago and there are hundreds of big stones and boulders covering about an acre of land. Lots of people were killed by the meteor, and are buried beneath the Stones."

"Ugh," Kristen exclaimed with a shiver, then hurriedly said, "I mean, big deal. So some unfortunate people got buried by a falling meteorite. What's that to got to do with *singing*, for pity's sake, and how does that make Friendly Corners haunted?"

I took up the tale, making my voice zombielike. "They say the spirits of the people buried under the Stones are desperate to get out. Lots of kids say that if you hit a certain stone or rock with a hammer, the spirits cry out—"

"*Sing*," Sean added with a ghoulish smile.

"Stones and singing and buried bodies," Kristen burst out, "it's just all nonsense. It's lame."

"Try telling that to Jamie Field," I said. "She insists that she accidentally hit one of the Singing Stones and unleashed a spirit. She says it chased her all the way into town."

"That's when the letters in the welcome sign changed," Sean added with relish. "Friendly Corners turned into Fiendly Corners."

Kristen made a panicky scuttling motion, but I blocked her path. Poking her in the back, I propelled her forward, closer to the entrance of the town square.

"Keep your eye on that *R* in the welcome sign," I gleefully instructed my cousin. "If it blinks off, let out a scream."

"Lame," Kristen mumbled under her breath as she took tiny steps forward. "This ghost stuff is a laugh." As if to prove how silly it was, she summoned her usual smirk. But it was a strained and almost frightened one.

"What's the matter?" I said with a smug smile. "Big brave Kristen scared of ghosts?"

"She's not afraid," Sean immediately piped up. "Kristen isn't afraid of anything."

We'll see about that, I thought in growing anticipation. Kristen was definitely making strange little sounds the closer we got to Main Street and the overhead sign. Not only that, she began to shiver, digging her hands into the pockets of her jacket after turning up the collar.

Come to think of it, it *was* growing uncomfortably chilly. The afternoon had been clear, cold and sunny, with just a pleasant nip in the air. As we got off the bridge, however, a damp mass of fog drifted in from the river. Like the pale figure of a ghost, it floated high over our heads and seemed to settle over the welcome sign.

"Do you see that?" Sean said in a shaky voice.

We stopped on the corner of Main Street, peering up into the chilly mist. I swallowed nervously and nodded. What was going on here? I thought.

Beside me, Kristen gave a little gasp and clutched at my arm.

"The letter *R*," she whispered. "I can't see it anymore. The *R* in the word Friendly disappeared!"

"No way," Sean said, but then shouted, "I see it, too! The sign reads Fiendly Corners." He wheeled around, jabbing at my shoulders in excitement. "Matt, do you see it?"

I squinted through the billowing mass of fog.

"I can't make out the letters," I exclaimed in frustration. "The fog's too thick."

I stared at the sign for a long breathless moment. The fog shifted for a moment, and I got a clear glimpse of the letters. I felt my knees go all rubbery. Incredible as it seemed, the reflectorized letters gleamed the word FIENDLY. The *R* had gone out, as if blocked by some invisible force.

Fiendly Corners.

A shiver prickled down my back.

"I see it," I whispered, then felt a tingle at the base of my neck. A cool little breeze tickled my skin and made me break out into goosebumps.

"*Matt . . . ,*" an eerie soft voice whispered in my ear. "*Don't go into Fiendly Corners . . . .*"

I froze, as if a snake had just slithered on the path in front of me.

"*Matt . . . ,*" the voice hissed.

A fingertip, rubbery and gross-feeling, pressed against my neck.

Muttering angrily, I wheeled around. Kristen was bending over me with Sean's rubber werewolf snout in her hand. She and my (now *definitely* former) best friend took one look at my face and broke out into helpless laughter.

"Oh, man, you should see yourself right now," Sean said, chortling in that dorky way of his.

"I'm not scared," I retorted coldly. "I was just caught off guard. You want *real* scared?" I asked Kristen. "You just wait. Next time I'll scare *you* more than you can scare me!"

Kristen snorted. "I dare you to try it, Matt."

"I'll take that dare," I said. But then I frowned. "Didn't you guys see the letter *R* blink off in the sign? You both said you did."

Sean shook his head, obviously puzzled. "Nothing happened to the sign. Kristen and I were just teasing you."

"But I saw it change!" I insisted.

"Sure you did," Kristen said with a disbelieving laugh. "You can stop trying to scare me with all that lame Fiendly Corners stuff, because I don't buy it. As if I'd be frightened of something that doesn't exist. For pity's sake, Matt, this sleepy little place is not haunted. And ghosts don't go around playing with the letters of the town name."

I gritted my teeth, but kept silent. I know what I saw. And no smirking attitude from the B Girl was going to change my mind. I took one look at that smug smiling face and vowed then and there to *terrify* Kristen Powers before her stay was over. My cousin had dared me to try it, and I would gladly accept the challenge—and win.

CHAPTER FOUR

We hurried through the Square with a number of other wannabe werewolves. It was obvious we were heading to the Palace for the matinee, but the people out shopping still turned to stare at us, pointing and laughing.

I didn't care. I had other things to think about—like the fact that I had seen the sign over Main Street change from FRIENDLY to FIENDLY CORNERS. I huffed and puffed behind Sean and Kristen, still visualizing the gleaming *R* blink mysteriously in the fog, then go out. I hadn't imagined it, had I? Hadn't wanted my cousin to witness the spooky side of town so desperately that I saw it only in my mind? I shook my head, frowning.

I caught up to Sean and Kristen. Sean was chattering nonstop, pointing out the town's local attractions.

"A square of four long blocks named after trees," Kristen was saying in her sarcastic voice. "Oak, Elm, Maple, and Pine. How original. And I love the old-fashioned lampposts. That must really cut down on crime after dark."

Okay, so our town wasn't life in the fast lane. It still had plenty going for it. Before Kristen left, I hoped she'd change her stuck-up little mind about Friendly Corners. (Or maybe the spirits in Fiendly Corners would change it for her.)

I tapped Sean's shoulder and motioned him away from my nosy cousin.

"Did you see the sign change, yes or no?" I asked him in a soft voice. "You've got to tell me the truth."

"I did tell you the truth and the answer is no," Sean sputtered indignantly. "I only said it goofing around."

I gripped the furry arm of his werewolf suit. "You didn't see the R blink off? Honestly?"

His face creased in his usual gloomy expression. "I wish I had. How come I never get to witness anything good and scary and other people do?"

"I saw it change," I told him. "But doesn't that mean that something's going to happen?"

We hadn't thought of that. Sean and I stared at each other, nervous and yet excited by the idea of ghosts. Because I was the one who had seen the words Fiendly Corners, did that mean a spirit would be coming after me? It was one thing to joke about the town's dark secret, quite another to play an active role in it. I felt a sinking coldness in my stomach. Maybe it wasn't such a bad idea to have the Fearless Wonder staying at our house for a few days. Just to be on the safe side, that is.

We cut across the park so Sean could touch the cannon in the middle of the Square. For some oddball reason he thought the old World War I cannon brought him luck, and today he needed a big dose to get a free pass to the show.

Kristen rolled her eyes at this superstitious display, so I blurted, "Dare you to jump over it."

Without giving it any thought, my cousin hurtled over the huge cannon as easily as if it had been a shoe box.

"Awesome," Sean said.

I clenched my teeth as we crossed onto Maple. The theater was on the corner, and there was a mob scene outside.

"That's the Palace?" Kristen said in disbelief. "You call that fossilized monstrosity the Palace?"

I stared at the three-story redbrick building with defensive pride. All right, so it wasn't the modern, glittering cineplex theater you find at malls or in big cities. The Palace was small and old-fashioned on the outside, but it had a wonderfully spooky horror mansion look inside. And you couldn't beat the special three-dollar admission.

"You wait," Sean told Kristen. "It's like a completely different world inside."

Kristen wrinkled her nose. "I just bet."

I turned on her. "If all this small-town stuff is below your high standards, then why did you want to come with us in the first place? Maybe you should run on home and keep your teddy bears company."

Bull's-eye. For a minute Kristen just stared at me. Her mouth opened and closed as if she were trying to come up with the perfect put-down, and then she smiled. It was a nice smile, the first genuine one I had seen from her, and it caught me off guard.

"I wanted to spend time with you," she said simply. "I never get a chance to see my favorite cousin."

Now *I* was speechless, and feeling pretty stupid. Had I been misjudging Kristen all along? Maybe we could be friends after all.

But then Kristen nudged me. "What's the matter? Cat got your tongue?"

Before I could stop her she began pinching me and tickling me around the waist and under my arms.

"Stop it!" I cried, embarrassed that the kids waiting in line would see (and hear) me explode into my wounded elephant snorts.

So much for our three-second truce.

I tried to wriggle out of her grip, and backed into someone.

"Well, well, Matt the Fat," said a voice I knew and dreaded.

Todd Slivack popped into view, a big, muscle-bound jerk with scraggly hair and the IQ of a potato chip. He motioned to his friends in the crowd.

"Hey, check it out," he crowed. "A Fatty Matty attack. And this time a girl's doing it."

As abruptly as she had grabbed me, Kristen let me go. She smiled and walked right up to Todd.

"What did you just say?" she asked in a strangely polite voice.

"What did you just say?" Todd mimicked her. "You heard me."

"I heard you call my cousin a name," she said, staring directly into Todd's eyes. She was looking at him as if he were a disgusting cockroach she couldn't wait to squash.

Todd snorted and tried to look away, but he couldn't seem to break Kristen's gaze.

"This fat tub is your cousin?" he said.

"That's right," Kristen said in that polite, cold voice. "And anyone who makes fun of a member of my family, makes fun of me. So are you calling me a fat tub?"

I groaned, waiting for the inevitable explosion. Was she certifiably insane? She practically signed my death warrant at that moment, daring to stand up to Todd. Now I was going to get it. Now *she* was going to get it.

"What are you, a black belt or something?" Todd jeered.

"Actually, she's getting her brown belt," Sean unexpectedly piped up.

Todd's jeer faded. Kristen put her hands on her hips as if to say, *I'm waiting*, and kept that cold, unblinking gaze on Todd. Incredibly, he gave a shrug, muttered, "She's crazy," and melted into the crowd.

Kristen turned back to me. "What an unbelievably obnoxious moron. I don't know why you put up with it."

"I enjoy living," I said, "you know, that thing called breathing."

"Kristen, you were something else," Sean said. "The way you intimidated Slivack."

"Yeah," I began, but couldn't find the words I needed to thank her. I was confused by my cousin's constant sarcasm, and then this turnabout to stand up for me. I guess I didn't understand Kristen at all.

Before I could worry too much about it, Commander Coffin appeared. Plump and round as a beach ball, with rosy pink cheeks, silvery hair, and a Santa Claus twinkle in his eyes, he looked about as much like his name as the Tooth Fairy. But the owner of the Palace loved horror movies and made it an experience to view the classics in his theater.

I noticed Kristen peering at Commander Coffin with a curl to her lip.

"Don't . . . say . . . a . . . word," I muttered.

"What?" she said in an injured voice. "I wasn't going to say anything."

In record time Coffin awarded free passes and handed out discount coupons for popcorn and candy. Kristen and I got in free (me for my two jokes and Kristen for a dynamite werewolf howl), while Sean had to pay.

"This is so typical," he groaned. "I never win *anything.*"

"Come on," Kristen said, "I'll treat you to popcorn."

I stood inside the lobby of the theater, watching Sean go off with my stuck-up cousin. Today was only Tuesday, for Pete's sake, and already Kristen had stolen my only friend and humiliated me in front of a crowd. What was she planning to do to me tomorrow and Thanksgiving? I shook my head, debating whether I wanted to wait in the long line with them for drinks and candy, or go find us seats.

I looked around the shadowy lobby, enjoying the creepy lighting in the shape of torches and the plush floor-to-ceiling red drapes. There were large prints of movie monsters hanging on the walls, and as an added touch, gruesome organ music played in the background. My home away from home, I thought with a smile. And too bad if Kristen makes fun of it. I decided I wasn't about to let her ruin what promised to be a fantastically terrifying werewolf double feature.

With that reassuring thought in mind, I stopped to tell Sean and Kristen I was going inside to save us seats and then I walked into the theater.

Something growled . . . .

Somewhere in the blackness, someone—or something—gave a low, throaty snarl.

I stopped immediately, looking around. Special effects like these had to come from Commander Coffin, who spent a lot of money making his matinees as spooky as possible.

Kids dressed as werewolves pushed past me, laughing and howling.

I let out a disappointed sigh. No special sound effects after all, just kids being funny and playing at being wolves. I began to march farther into the cavernous theater.

33

There, behind me, another savage growl.

This was no kid playing at monsters, I realized. This had to be Commander Coffin's doing. I snapped my fingers, hitting upon a brilliant scheme. Maybe if I got Commander Coffin to agree, he'd let me "borrow" the tape (or whatever made the realistic snarls) to put a king-size scare into Kristen.

"Hey, move it," two boys impatiently shouted. Startled, I turned aside to let them pass and bumped into a man standing right behind me. Frail and ancient-looking, his cobwebby white hair haloed a face crisscrossed in wrinkles. Yet his eyes, an eerie yellow color, stared into mine with frightening intensity. He leaned close to me, a bony finger pointed at my startled face. In a black double-breasted suit and dark beret, he reminded me of an undertaker. "You heard those howls," he whispered in a faintly accented voice. "I know you heard them."

Slightly nervous, I backed a few inches away and nodded.

The savage growls came again.

Turning on his heel so quickly I jumped, the man scuttled toward the lobby like a lizard chasing his prey.

Creepy, I thought with a shudder, but I had to make tracks, too. I wanted to find Commander Coffin before the double feature started to ask him about those awesome sounds. The sounds that would scare Kristen to death.

I bumped into Sean and Kristen in the lobby, their arms loaded with popcorn, candy, and sodas.

"What's up?" Sean said. "I thought you were finding us seats."

"I was," I said, "but something more important came up. I need to talk to Commander Coffin first. So you guys save me a seat, okay?"

Ignoring their puzzled faces and questions, I rushed up the carpeted stairs to the balcony. Commander Coffin had closed the balcony for safety reasons, but his tiny office was located on the second floor landing.

The door to the office was slightly ajar. I paused outside, wondering if Commander Coffin would be annoyed at me for bothering him before a double feature.

I hesitated, not sure what to do, when I heard the sound of raised voices.

Something thudded against the door. I gave a startled gasp, and took a step back.

Too late. The door swung open. A creature covered in fur (half man, half wolf) glared at me with wild animal eyes. His lips twisted back from yellowish, pointed fangs.

Werewolf, I thought, as I tried to scream but nothing came out of my throat.

CHAPTER FIVE

I tripped over my feet, trying to back away.

The thing—the *werewolf*—edged closer.

That's when I saw plump, pink fingers curling around its furry body and twinkling blue eyes appearing over its head.

Commander Coffin was carrying a life-size cardboard cutout of a werewolf out of his office. *Trying* to carry it out, that is. A man was in the office with him, grabbing on to his arm and pleading with him. I blinked, recognizing the man as the creepy person who spoke to me in the theater minutes ago.

"You cannot, should not, put this image on display," the man was insisting. "You'll only be asking for trouble."

The man was whispering in that soft, accented voice, yet there was a threat in his words. He was staring at Commander Coffin with those chilly yellow eyes. Neither of the two men noticed me as I awkwardly stood in the hall.

Commander Coffin gave his head an irritated shake.

"I'm sorry, Mr. Gerkas—"

"Cherkas," the man corrected him. "Victor Cherkas."

"I don't see any harm in putting up a posterboard like this to advertise for our next feature. I do it all the time for my other films."

"But this is no ordinary film," Cherkas said. *"The*

Night of the Hairy Horror has a disturbing history, as you well know."

"*The Hairy Horror?*" I blurted with a kind of awe in my voice. "You're going to be showing *The Hairy Horror?*"

I forgot my embarrassment in eavesdropping on this private argument. I couldn't believe my ears. *The Night of the Hairy Horror*, a werewolf film made in 1958, had supposedly been so realistically gruesome that audience members fainted and screamed at the first previews. The movie was subsequently pulled for editing and cutting, but was never released in the end. Apparently the lead actor playing the hairy horror had tragically fallen to his death while filming new scenes in Romania. The director and various members of the cast had also mysteriously died or were involved in accidents on location.

"*The Hairy Horror*," I murmured again. "Radical."

Both men turned to stare at me, Commander Coffin startled and slightly annoyed, Victor Cherkas frowning.

"I can't believe it," I went on, ignoring the impatience on Commander Coffin's face. "Wait until I tell Sean about this. You don't know Sean. You wouldn't believe his collection of—"

"You wanted something, Matt?" Commander Coffin cut me off.

"Oh, uh, yeah," I mumbled, momentarily forgetting the reason I had come to his office after learning this exciting news.

"Well, what is it?" Coffin demanded. "I'm right in the middle of something."

As if to emphasize the point, the theater owner banged the cutout on the floor.

I shifted awkwardly under the reptile stare of Cherkas. "Downstairs in the theater," I began, "I heard

37

these wonderful growling noises, and savage snarls. Terrific sound effects, and I wanted to ask you—"

"Growling noises?" Coffin said in a disbelieving voice. "Savage snarls? Is this some kind of joke?"

"No," I said. "And you don't need to act like you don't know what I'm talking about. I promise I won't tell anybody about the werewolf-like sound effects if I could just talk to you about borrowing your tape or CD to use on a friend. I know the sounds would scare her. Hey, they even gave me the chills for a minute, they were so real."

"But that's impossible," Commander Coffin said. His bushy white eyebrows shot up. "I didn't use any sound effects for this show. So if you heard growling, someone must have snuck their pet dog into the theater and I won't allow that."

"It wasn't a pet," I insisted, confused and a little nervous. "If you had heard those growls you'd know it wasn't anyone's dog."

"Well, then, what could it be, Matt?" Coffin said. He thought for a moment, frowning, then gave a relieved laugh. "You heard the kids howling. That's what the mystery sound was. Some of them howled more like werewolves than the movie version. Now, if you'll excuse me . . ." He hoisted the life-size cutout in his hands.

"But it wasn't the kids," I said stubbornly. I shook my head. "No *person* could growl like that."

Victor Cherkas stepped forward, eyes glinting strangely.

"What made the sound then?"

He pressed against the door, as still and yet alert as a lizard on a rock. If I gave the wrong answer, would he unexpectedly pounce on me?

I let out a frustrated groan. "I don't know, I keep

telling you. But there's something inside this theater."

Commander Coffin squeezed his eyes shut as if begging for mercy, then propped the werewolf cutout against the wall of his office.

"All right, Matt, you've convinced me. I'm going downstairs to check on this matter." He turned to Victor Cherkas. "I'll see you out, as well. I believe our discussion is over."

But the strange-looking man refused to budge. He pressed his lips together, and angrily shook his head. "It's not over," he said in an eerie whisper. "As long as you insist on showing *The Night of the Hairy Horror*, then you must be told about the curse."

"Oh, for heaven's sake, not that outdated story again," Commander Coffin said. He let out an explosive sound like an angry laugh. "First you come in here, claiming to be the special effects person who worked on the *Hairy Horror* film and insist I hand over the cardboard cutout of the werewolf. Now you tell me there's a curse on showing the movie, as well. I must tell you, sir, that I've heard all the rumors and stories about this movie. They don't frighten me."

"But they should," Cherkas said bitterly. "Many people, my coworkers, died working on that film. I know that for a fact. I was there."

"Unfortunate accidents happen," Coffin said. He spread his hands wide and frowned. "People have died on other movie sets, as well. Does that mean I'm going to be tempting fate if I show this movie in my theater? You can't possibly believe this curse, or jinx, is real. After all these years?"

"Do not show *The Night of the Hairy Horror*," Cherkas repeated in a half whisper. "A Romanian Gypsy placed a curse on the movie because the director decided to film scenes on her family's land, sacred ground she claimed. I am Romanian and I tell you now, you cannot fight this curse. It reaches out, even across a great distance, almost forty years later."

Cool, I thought. This was going to make a great story to tell Sean and Kristen, complete with vengeful Gypsies, ancient curses, and unusual deaths.

A smile twitched at my lips as I envisioned Sean's reaction.

But Victor Cherkas (the Lizard Man) poked a withered finger in my face. His eyes were narrowed and cold. I shivered despite myself.

"Be warned, young friend. *You* heard the beast stirring. *You* heard its growls. The Hairy Horror is alive, and is haunting this theater."

"Now just a minute," Commander Coffin indignantly sputtered, rounding on Cherkas. "Don't try to frighten the boy with your own silly superstitions. I think we've heard quite enough for one day."

Cherkas pointedly ignored Commander Coffin. His yellow eyes never left my face.

"I am going, never fear. But if you need my help, as I think you will, I'll be staying at the Riverside Inn at the foot of the bridge."

And with a twisted grimace, Cherkas turned on his heel and scuttled out of the office.

Commander Coffin made a snorting sound.

"What a character," he exclaimed. "Crazy."

"Crazy," I echoed.

I peered inside the office at the life-size cutout. Even from a distance, the fur-covered body seemed alive and ready to pounce. The glistening snout with its sharpened

40

fangs growled in my imagination. The red-rimmed eyes, trapped and savage, impaled mine with blazing intensity.

"The Hairy Horror is alive," Victor Cherkas had said.

Ridiculous, I quickly thought. The Hairy Horror was a movie monster, in the same company as Dracula, Frankenstein, and the Wolf Man. No more real than Santa Claus or the Easter Bunny.

Then who—or what—had made the growling noises earlier?

Don't think about it, I commanded myself. There must be a logical explanation.

As I followed Commander Coffin down the stairs to the lobby, I got the glimmer of a brilliant idea. It had to do with my (supposedly) fearless cousin and the Singing Stones.

But the best part of all involved the Hairy Horror.

Before the night was over Kristen would be howling again—this time in fear.

CHAPTER SIX

The sun had gone down by the time we came out of the
theater. All the kids went to Roba's on the Square for the
best pizza in town, so the three of us ended up in a corner
booth, sharing a jumbo pepperoni-and-mushroom pizza.

"I dare you to eat more than four slices," I taunted
Kristen, who had devoured a tub of popcorn and several
candy bars during the show.

"And I dare you to eat less than two!" she retorted.

I muttered under my breath, but vowed to do it.
Luckily I had ordered a big helping of french fries on the
side.

"Speaking of dares," I said, "I dare you to go to the
Stones tonight. Yes or no?"

Kristen quirked an eyebrow as she tore off a slice of
pizza. "Let me finish eating and I'll give you my answer."

I held my breath, waiting. Everything depended
upon Kristen's answer. If she said yes, then I'd finally
prove to Sean what a big phony she was. Because what I
intended to do to her up at Singing Stones would terrify
the life out of anybody—even her stunt pilot parents.

I peered out the front window of Roba's, nervously
tapping my fingers on the table. It was now six o'clock
and already dark. The Square had a dead look, despite
the flickering glow from the lampposts and illuminated
shop fronts. A wind had kicked up and was tossing the

skeletal branches of trees together. The branches made a rattling sound, like bony fingers clawing at a closed coffin lid.

A perfect night for ghost hunting at the Singing Stones, I thought, mentally rubbing my hands together in glee. To make it even spookier, a full moon was rising in the sky.

I stared over at my cousin, cramming the fifth slice of pepperoni-and-mushroom pizza into her mouth. In between bites, she was bragging about her skills in karate, claiming how she'd won various competitions. Across the table, Sean was rattling ice cubes in his soda and hanging on to every word. I picked up the salt shaker and banged it down on the tabletop.

"Hey!" Sean exclaimed, nearly knocking over his glass.

"I'm waiting for an answer," I said, staring at Kristen. "Do you have the guts to go to the Singing Stones or not?"

Kristen swallowed the last bite of her pizza, then ever so carefully and slowly wiped her fingers with the napkin. All the while her mouth was curving in that smug little smile I hated. She wouldn't say no, would she? It would be just like my contrary cousin to say or do the unexpected.

I sat like a lump, shoulders hunched, waiting for her response. I was so keyed up I couldn't finish the last of my buttered french fries.

She paused another agonizing moment and then said, "Of course I'll go. You think I'm scared of some stupid Singing Stones? Or of anything else in your bogus haunted town?"

I lowered my voice and said, "You should be scared. Look what happened in the Palace this afternoon."

Kristen flipped back a strand of long hair and snorted. "Oh, right. The Hairy Horror saga. The curse of the Gypsy on some old movie that was never released and creepy toad Victor Jerk-man—"

"Cherkas," I corrected her coldly.

"Whatever." She continued, "Victor warns you the werewolf is alive and haunting the theater."

"Snicker all you want," I responded nastily. "It's true. Every last word. I *did* hear strange growls inside the theater."

"But no one found anything," Kristen said. "Commander Coffin found zilch."

"Just because no one found evidence of the cause of the sounds doesn't mean it wasn't real. I heard it with my own ears. I didn't imagine it."

"Just like he saw the sign change in town," Sean added. He scowled. "Cool things are always happening to Matt, and nothing great ever happens to me."

Kristen's lips twitched. "I forgot about the letters magically turning into Fiendly Corners. Your imagination has certainly been working overtime today, Matt."

I glared at Kristen, but she smiled at me.

"You really want your town to be haunted," she said. "You and Sean are like little kids playing a game of make-believe."

"We'll see who the little kid is tonight," I warned her. "We'll see who runs screaming in the dark at the Singing Stones."

Kristen hooted softly and stood up. "You've got to stop going to horror movies, little cousin. You're starting to believe in fantasy. Now if you'll excuse me, I'm going to the ladies' room."

She spun on her heel to leave, then abruptly leaned

over the table. "Don't let any vampires take my seat while I'm gone."

Sean chortled appreciatively as Kristen left.

I shot a stream of soda at him through my straw. The cola hit him directly on the nose and dripped down onto his werewolf suit.

"Hey," he whined, wiping his face. "Why did you go and do that? This costume needs to be returned tomorrow morning and I don't want stains on it."

"Then quit laughing that doofus laugh whenever the Queen Bee says something," I retorted. "Cut it out. You want her already-swollen head to grow even fatter?"

"Her head looks fine to me," Sean said, rubbing the fur with a napkin. "You're the one with the problem."

"Man, she has you wrapped around her little finger. Talking tough, acting so brave." I poked my straw in his face. "You wait until she's up at the Singing Stones. She won't be so tough and brave then."

Sean tapped nervously on the table. "Are you sure this is such a good idea? Acting out our own little version of the Night of the Hairy Horror on Kristen? What if she freaks on us?"

"That's the whole point," I said with a grin. "And I don't want you going soft and getting mushy on me, because Kristen Powers doesn't deserve it."

"Well . . ." Sean scrunched up his freckled face, obviously torn between his loyalty to me and his silly crush on Kristen.

"Besides," I hurriedly added, "we've wanted to see proof of Friendly Corners being haunted for a long time. Today I saw the sign change. I heard those growls in the Palace. Maybe we'll both see a real ghost tonight at the Singing Stones."

"A ghost," Sean whispered in a dreamy voice. "I'd give *anything* to see that."

"All right then," I said, banging the table for emphasis. "No more talking about wimping out on our plan. I had to practically beg my parents to let Kristen eat dinner with us in town and I had to plead with Commander Coffin to loan us the cardboard cutout of the Horror—"

"Yeah, well I had to grovel to get my brother to agree to drive us to the Stones," Sean interrupted. "Not to mention stopping by the Palace first to pick up the cutout and then hiding it in his van. He's charging me a percentage of my allowance, you know."

"It'll be worth it," I said. I chuckled inside, thinking of Kristen's terrified reaction when she saw—and heard—a real werewolf in the dark. "Hey, be quiet. She's coming back. Now not a word about the Hairy Horror cutout or the tape John's bringing. It's all got to be a big surprise."

"I just hope nothing goes wrong," Sean muttered in a pessimistic voice. "With my track record something *always* gets screwed up."

Kristen slid into the booth and stared suspiciously at us. "Something going on?" she asked.

I was all set to make a glib comment, when something caught my eye. A dark shadowy figure pressed against the window of Roba's. Peering into the pizza place with cupped hands. Searching for someone.

Victor Cherkas, I realized with a lurch of my stomach. He caught my startled eye and held it for a nerve-rattling moment. His piercing gaze made it seem as if he could read my mind. As if he knew what I was planning to do at the Singing Stones. Me—and the Hairy Horror.

"Outside the window," I managed to croak. "It's Cherkas!"

"What?" Sean exclaimed. He and Kristen immediately turned to look over their shoulders, but the Lizard Man was gone. Vanished into the darkness of the Square.

When Sean's brother pulled up to Roba's seconds later and impatiently beeped for us, I couldn't rush out fast enough. Was the Lizard Man following me for some reason? I wondered as I scrambled into the van with Kristen and Sean.

I was getting a weird feeling about tonight. But I couldn't back down now.

We were all quiet on the drive to the Ridge.

Kristen hummed tunelessly under her breath, as if to let me know how childish this dare was. Sean nibbled his lower lip, shooting me worried glances. Sean's seventeen-year-old brother John sang along with some loud grunge band on the radio.

I huddled against the passenger door of the van, staring out at the countryside. We had left the cozy lights of town behind us and were heading into the densely wooded area of the Ridge. John made the turnoff for the Singing Stones and we began to climb. Trees grew thicker along the side of the twisting, narrow lane. There were no streetlights in this desolate area, but an icy yellow moon illuminated the darkness.

I peered up at the full moon and grinned.

Talk about a perfect setting for a werewolf sighting. All my planning was going to pay off, I thought. I hadn't had much time to prepare, but now it was coming together. If Sean played his part correctly, Kristen would be howling for her teddy bears in less than ten minutes or so. And I wouldn't have to put up with my cousin's bragging ever again. She'd be exposed for the phony she was.

The van bumped along for a few minutes on the country road and then crawled to a stop along the dirt shoulder. John turned off the radio and looked at us.

"End of the line," he said.

The three of us tumbled out of the van and huddled in the cold. Kristen peered into the darkness with a frown.

"We're in the middle of nowhere," she complained. "I don't see any Singing Stones."

I pointed out an almost invisible trail with a chained entrance.

"It's inside there," I explained in a spooky voice. "Deep inside the woods."

It was quiet up here. As silent and as deserted as a cemetery at midnight. The wind had died down, so nothing disturbed the unearthly stillness.

"Wait!" Kristen exclaimed, holding up a hand. "What was that?"

We strained to listen. Far off in the underbrush twigs snapped.

"An animal," John offered in a bored voice. "Rabbit or squirrel."

"Or a spirit . . ." Sean whispered.

Perfect, I mentally crowed. Talk about setting the stage. I leaned inside the interior of the van and pulled out two items. "Flashlight and hammer," I said, holding them up. "Can't summon a ghost without them."

Kristen rolled her eyes. "This is so lame. But at least I'll have some funny stories to tell my friends when I get back to school."

"We'll see who's laughing in a few minutes," I said, and nodded toward the entrance. "Ready to visit the Stones?"

"Oh, for pity's sake, let's just go in there and get it over with," my cousin retorted. Tossing her hair, she briskly marched to the entrance and slipped beneath the chain.

"Hey!" I called. "Wait for me!"

Mumbling last minute instructions to Sean, I hurried to catch up with her.

CHAPTER SEVEN

"Kristen, come back here!" I angrily hissed.

I scrambled under the chain and caught up to my cousin. She was creeping along the gravel path at a snail's pace.

"Hold on a minute," I ordered, fumbling with the switch on the flashlight. It was dark inside the entrance to the Stones, dark and utterly silent. Tall, twisted trees formed a heavy canopy over our heads and blocked the full moon. A chilly mist rose from the ground, skeleton pale in color and damp. It swirled along the path and drifted among the trees.

I had been up here many times before, lots of time at night, but somehow it felt different—*strange*—this evening. Almost as if something was lurking in the bushes, watching us.

But that was crazy, I thought quickly. I was letting my imagination run away with me. First hearing those growls in the Palace theater and then spotting Victor Cherkas outside Roba's front window. If anyone was going to be scared at the Singing Stones, it would be my cousin, Kristen "I Dare You" Powers.

I finally clicked the flashlight on and shined the narrow light on the path.

"Let's go," I said in a hushed and creepy voice. "The spirits await us."

Kristen began to sway in front of me like a ghost, waving her arms and moaning.

"The spirits are calling us," she wailed. "Help them to escape, Matthew. Help them float down to the town so they can turn Friendly Corners into *Fiendly Corners*."

"Laugh all you want," I snapped. "You'll stop as soon as you see the Stones."

Kristen stopped swaying and jeered. "Right. The famous Singing Stones. I can't wait."

"All right then," I announced in an exasperated voice. "Let's go. And stay in front of me so I don't lose you. It's a little difficult to see with all this mist."

I started down the path but Kristen grabbed my arm. "Wait a minute. Where's Sean? Shouldn't we wait for him?"

I blinked at her, trying to come up with a good excuse. "Uh, he'll join us in a few minutes. He has to straighten something out with his brother."

"Odd," she said, wrinkling her nose. "I thought that you and he went everywhere together. I'm surprised you don't wear pagers to keep track of each other all day."

"Ha-ha," I said coldly. "Sean and I are big boys who can get along without each other perfectly easily. Perhaps *you're* the one who needs Sean by your side, holding your hand." I smiled at her. "If you're too scared to go to the Stones without Sean, we can wait for him."

"Oh, for pity's sake," Kristen said, throwing up her hands, "let's just go. Let's get this little ghost game of yours over with. But before we do," she added with a smirk, "I dare you to turn off the flashlight so we have to walk in the dark."

I stared at her, reluctant to agree but hating to show any fear. That infuriating curl to her lip made me snap off the light.

51

"Fine," I muttered, "and I dare you to lead the way."

She hesitated for a second, then grinned like a jack-o'-lantern on Halloween night.

"You're on," she giggled, then playfully shoved me. "But let's see who begs for a light first."

"It won't be me," I snorted.

We picked our way along the gravel path, tripping over weeds and large roots. As much as I despised my cousin's bossiness and daredevil front, I had to give her credit. Not once did she falter or hesitate as we walked in the dark. Of course, I realized, she didn't know what was waiting for her just around the bend. My lips twitched a little, anticipating the look of horror on her face when she got her first glimpse of the Hairy Horror.

I didn't even have to wait that long for a reaction.

The moment we edged through an opening in the trees and spotted the clearing, Kristen froze. She made a faint sound in her throat, but couldn't say a word. I grinned beside her. The Singing Stones almost always produced a shocked silence in first time viewers. Not only because the acre of land was crowded with stones and rocks the shape and color of tombstones, but also because of the trees. Rotted, misshapen stumps stood watch over the clearing with seemingly evil intent. They looked like witches' hats poking up into the sky. In addition, an almost phosphorescent mist swirled out of the rocks, like ghosts trying desperately to escape.

The Singing Stones was no ordinary place. It was a cemetery of sorts, with rocks and boulders serving as graves. Know-it-all people like my cousin could make fun of the Stones, but once they came here, once they experienced the eerie sensations firsthand, they no longer laughed.

Kristen wasn't laughing. She took an uncertain step closer and stared out at the Stones.

I leaned over her shoulder. "What's the matter?" I asked. "No smart comments or jokes?"

"Ssshhhhh!" Kristen abruptly held up her hand. "I hear something!"

One thing it couldn't be was Sean. He had his instructions and knew full well to wait for his cue. I hadn't given him that so Kristen must have heard something else.

"What is it?" I whispered.

She gazed out over the Stones, eyes widening in alarm. Her normally smirking face looked scared and drawn in the moonlight.

"Kristen, what is it?" I repeated, beginning to get nervous despite myself. If the Fearless Wonder was quivering beside me, then something must be wrong.

"I don't know," she said with a shrug. "I just felt for a second that someone—or something—was out there in all those trees. Pretty dumb, huh?"

Not so dumb at all, I thought with a smirk. The Hairy Horror was lurking in the woods and Sean was going to bring him to life in a very short while. I couldn't wait to see the expression on my cousin's face when he appeared.

"Now that you mention it," I whispered, "I get the same crawly sensation, too." I shivered inside my flannel jacket, pretending to be nervous. "Maybe we should call it a night and just go on home."

"Absolutely not," Kristen protested, just as I knew she would. "Nothing is going to scare me away from these stupid Stones."

I threw up my hands. "Okay, then. Let's see who's been right all along about the trapped spirits when you hit one of the Stones." I shoved the hammer in front of her startled face. "Go on, Miss I-Dare-You," I said loudly. "Make the Stones sing."

That was Sean's cue. Be alert, be ready. I had instructed him to wait a few moments after Kristen and I entered the clearing, then quietly follow us in. Right at this very moment he should be hiding behind some trees close to where we were standing, Hairy Horror cutout in hand. He also should be ready to turn on the tape recorded special effects of screams and savage howls when he heard me give a certain line.

Please don't mess this up, Sean, I mentally urged my friend. Don't create one of your natural disasters tonight.

Kristen grabbed the hammer out of my hand, jolting me back to the present.

"Hey, wait!" I nervously shouted. "You can't go tapping the Stones without saying the words."

She stared at me. "What words? Like something out of a magic spell?"

"Just the *right* words," I said with emphasis. "The words that other kids have used to make the Stones sing." (I was lying, of course. There were no special words, but I needed to have Sean listen to certain phrases in order to make his entrance at the right moment.)

"Oh, for pity's sake," Kristen burst out, then nodded as if to humor me. "All right, Matt, if it'll make you feel better, if it's part of your little ghost game."

"It's no game," I snapped. "You just wait."

"Just tell me the words to say," Kristen sighed.

I raised my voice so Sean could hear me. "Listen carefully," I instructed Kristen. "You say: 'I take this hammer, I strike this stone, I make it sing, to bring the spirits home.' You got that?"

Frowning, Kristen shoved the hammer at me. "You do it first."

"What's the matter," I asked, "chicken?"

"I'll do it after you," Kristen repeated.

I gripped the hammer, said the words, and gently tapped a smallish stone hidden beneath two large boulders.

The stone vibrated, then gave off an unearthly peal. It shattered the stillness like an eerie wail.

"*Mat-the-e-e-w . . .* " it seemed to call.

"Whoa," Kristen murmured, eyes widening in shock.

I felt a shiver prickle down my back.

She and I stared at each other, then she yanked the hammer out of my nerveless fingers.

"Let me hit it!" she cried. She struck the stone with incredible force. Nothing happened except for the dull sound of impact. No peal, no ghostly wail.

"Do it again, Matt," she urged me. She shoved the hammer into my hand. "Make it sing again!"

I stared down at the hammer. Had I really made one of the Stones sing? Had I accidentally unleashed a spirit?

Before I could repeat the ritual, Kristen grabbed my arm. "Something's out there. I just saw something."

Another of my cousin's tricks? I immediately thought, but then I heard a crashing sound. Twigs snapped with sharp explosions as something hurtled through the woods. The full moon threw its icy brilliance on the clearing, creating spooky shadows. I peered into the darkness, and made out a black shape, waiting behind some trees.

Sean the werewolf, I thought with a giggle, and boy, was he making a terrifying but great first impression.

I pointed a phonily shaking finger. "Over there."

But the thing that edged out into the moonlight was no cardboard cutout of a werewolf, flat and one dimensional.

This black shape was long, low, and lean, with demon-red eyes. Raging eyes that gleamed in the darkness as if searching for something.

Where was Sean? I thought in confused panic.

What in the world was going on?

The wolflike beast appeared. The fanged mouth opened and gave a low throaty snarl.

The same snarl I had heard earlier in the Palace Theater.

"Werewolf," I whispered in blind panic. *"Werewolf!"*

The flashlight dropped from my shaking hand as the beast settled into a crouch and prepared to spring!

CHAPTER EIGHT

I froze in terror, too shocked to scream.

Beside me Kristen dug her fingernails in my arm. "What kind of a dog is that?" she exclaimed in fascinated horror. "I've never seen one that big!"

My jaw dropped. "Are you crazy? That's a *wolf*, for Pete's sake. Not some harmless Pekingese or poodle!"

"Then let's move," Kristen announced coolly, and spun on her heel.

I stumbled in my desperation to escape and tripped over Kristen's boots. Together we collapsed on the Stones in a tangled heap.

I jerked my head up—and looked over at the rage-inflamed eyes of the wolf.

Although still in the shadows, I could tell it was a big animal, bigger than any normal dog or wolf, maybe one hundred and fifty pounds. It was the spitting image of the cutout of the Hairy Horror, but unlike the cutout, this werewolf was alive. It looked straight in my direction and let out a howl, long, desperate—and hungry.

I'm going to die, I thought in desperation. *Gobbled alive by a werewolf.*

With a screaming snarl, the beast launched itself through the clearing and charged.

I covered my face with my hands, waiting for the force of impact.

It never came.

The werewolf sailed over our heads like a dark comet and thundered into the edge of the woods on the other side.

There was a crashing sound and a piercing cry.

Someone—or something—had gotten in the way of the creature. The stillness of the Singing Stones dissolved into shouts, screams, and snarls.

Without warning, all was quiet.

Kristen and I uncovered our heads and exchanged wild-eyed glances.

"What was *that*?" Kristen said.

"Werewolf, I told you," I babbled in panic. "The Hairy Horror! And I think it's found Sean!"

We jumped up, not even noticing our collective scrapes and bruises from the jagged rocks.

"We've got to find him," I cried, grabbing Kristen's arms. "Sean's been attacked by a werewolf!"

"The sounds came from over there," Kristen said, pointing to the area of woods where the werewolf had vanished.

"It's my fault," I mumbled, half running, half stumbling with Kristen over the boulders and stones. "It's all my fault."

"Don't be ridiculous," Kristen snapped, but she didn't know the half of it. If I hadn't thought up this fur-brained scheme to scare my cousin, we would never have come to the Stones. I never would have tapped a rock and unleashed the evil—what? spirit? ghost? werewolf?— that chased after Sean. My friend would still be all right, I thought in guilty horror, not lying in the woods after an attack. Sean could very well be . . .

Don't think it, I told myself as we frantically hurried through the clearing.

A shape tore out of the woods, just as we were about to rush in.

I gave a frightened yelp and backed into Kristen.

"Hey, it's me, it's Sean," the figure said, holding up his hands.

"Sean, are you all right?' Kristen cried, pulling him into the moonlight to examine him. "Did that crazy animal hurt you?"

"What animal?" Sean said, scrunching up his face in confusion. "What are you guys talking about?"

"No time to talk now," I snapped. "We've got to get out of here. The werewolf could still be around."

Sean issued that dorky laugh, and bared imaginary fangs. "Oh, yeah, right, a werewolf. Now I know you two are kidding."

"Matthew swears a killer werewolf's after us," Kristen explained, "but it looked like a big dog to me."

"Didn't you hear it howling?" I angrily shouted. "That animal was no dog. Now let's not stand around here chatting until it decides to attack again."

I grabbed both Kristen's and Sean's arms and pushed them toward the path. The quicker we left the Stones, the safer we'd be, I thought. Somehow I didn't think the evil spirit would be able to follow us out.

"You don't have to shove," Sean whined, stumbling along in the dark.

I had no flashlight. I had dropped it in the clearing when I first spotted the werewolf. I had no hammer. That, too, had been left behind in my fright. Terrific, I thought nervously, as we torturously scrambled our way along the shadowy, tree-lined path. Low-hanging branches slapped at our faces. Twisted thick roots shot up from the ground and tripped us. And all the while the ghostlike mist swirled in front of us, making it difficult to see. It was quiet, eerily quiet, as dark and deserted as an Egyptian tomb. I couldn't even make out the comforting sound of frogs and crickets. My heart was drumming too wildly in my chest. But something was lurking in the shadows, red eyes glowing. Something was snarling like far-off thunder inside my head. A splinter of cold pricked the back of my neck and I knew the werewolf was watching . . . waiting. At any moment it would jump out of the underbrush, razor sharp claws extended.

The Hairy Horror, I thought, my teeth beginning to chatter.

I don't know how I had done it—tapping the stone, saying the magic words, or simply being up here under a full moon—but somehow, some way, I had unleashed a force. A force that assumed the shape of the Hairy Horror.

I had heard the stone wail in the night.

I had heard it "sing" my name.

Now whatever was out there was looking for me, coming after me.

A twig snapped in the underbrush and a voice inside me shouted, *Run! Now!* I shoved a startled Kristen and Sean to the end of the trail and pushed them beneath the chain of the entrance.

"We're safe out here," I murmured, heart pounding wildly. "Nothing can touch us."

I peered into the moonlit shadows. "The van's gone! I thought John was going to wait for us."

"Relax," Sean said. "He'll be back. Knowing my brother, he's just cruising around, killing time."

I bent over, panting like a dog, as Kristen and Sean stared at me.

"Man, you are really losing it," Sean said, gasping

for air as well. "Going this far to scare Kristen."

"I'm not scared," Kristen immediately announced, and then stiffened. "What do you mean, going this far? Going this far *how*?"

"Well, you know," Sean blurted with a grin, "the Hairy Horror Plan. Getting you up to the Stones to set the mood, and then pretending to show you a werewolf."

I groaned inside, waggling my fingers to silence Sean. Too late. The damage had been done.

Kristen whipped her head around to stare at me. Her eyes glittered dangerously in the moonlight.

"The Hairy Horror Plan?" she repeated in an icy voice. "Perhaps you better explain."

I croaked a phony laugh. "It's nothing," I said. "Sean meant the Singing Stones ritual, that's all. He just got confused because he's scared."

"I'm not scared," Sean insisted with a baffled scowl. "And I'm not confused. You told me to carry the Hairy Horror cutout with me into the Stones and then at a certain cue, play the taped growls and run by with the werewolf cutout. You remember, Matt. You set it all up after the movie."

I shook my head, trying to deny the obvious, but Kristen wasn't buying it.

"Crazy," I muttered, pointing at Sean. "I don't see any cutout, so I guess—"

I stopped short, realizing what I just said.

"I don't see any cutout," I hissed. "What happened to the cutout? You know where it is, right?"

I stared at Sean in openmouthed horror when he shook his head.

"It's a funny thing," he began, but it didn't sound funny to me. It didn't sound funny at all. "Well," he continued, scratching his head, "I put it down beside a clump of trees and left it for a few minutes while I watched you guys by the Stones. You know, I was listening for my cue—"

"Cue?" Kristen exploded. "What cue?"

I shushed her. "Not now," I shouted, then lowered my voice. "Go on, Sean. You left it for a few moments and then what?"

"Well, I heard you say the words, 'Make the Stones sing,' so I hurried back to get it, but when I got to the trees, it was gone. Poof! Disappeared. That's why I was running to tell you, but you interrupted me with all this werewolf talk."

"It's there," I murmured, crossing my fingers. "It's got to be there. You just went to to the wrong place. Sure, that's it. If we go back to look, we'll find it.'

But Sean was staring at me with that doom-and-gloom expression on his freckled face. "I knew I'd ruin everything. And I'd miss everything, too. You guys both saw that monster dog—"

"Werewolf," I corrected through clenched teeth.

"—and I was nowhere close."

"Don't forget to tell Sean about the stone that 'sang,' as well," Kristen added with a smirk. "But it was all a setup, wasn't it? To get me to lose it." She poked a finger in my startled face. "But I didn't lose it, did I, Matt? It was a good joke, arranging for that eerie sound to come out of the stone, and renting that stupid big dog—"

"Werewolf," I shouted angrily. "It was a real werewolf. And that stone I tapped 'sang' for real. I'm in trouble, in case you don't know it. Big trouble."

"Because we lost Commander Coffin's cutout?" Sean asked innocently.

I stared at him, suddenly putting two and two together and coming up with a scary answer.

Fear tickled my spine.

"Victor Cherkas warned us about the Hairy Horror and the old Gypsy curse," I said in a small, frightened whisper. "But I didn't listen. I took the cutout up here to the Stones, under a full moon no less, and tapped one of the rocks. Somehow, and I don't know why, that cutout turned into the Hairy Horror."

I expelled a painfully held breath as I turned and gazed into the darkness of the woods.

"And now the werewolf's coming after *me*!"

CHAPTER NINE

The van pulled up, shattering the quiet with John's music. John motioned us inside, but I hesitated. Shouldn't we return to the Stones to search for the cutout? I thought I heard a low snarl coming from the bushes. Whether real or imaginary, that decided the matter for me. No way would I enter those dark woods if the werewolf were still around. Besides, I thought, hopping into the van with Kristen and Sean, if my suspicions were true, the cutout would *not* be there. The Hairy Horror would be prowling under a full moon, very much alive and real.

I shivered, despite the warm air blasting from the heater.

Here I had gone to the Singing Stones to terrify the teddy bears out of Kristen, and I was the one who was frightened out of my wits.

Of course, no one believed me. We sat in the van, talking with soft voices so John wouldn't hear us. "Quit going on about the Singing Stones and werewolves, for pity's sake," Kristen said sarcastically. "From now on I'm calling Fiendly Corners 'Funny Corners.'"

Sean snorted in that doofus way and then poked me. "Are you sure the Stones sang for you?" he asked repeatedly, wrinkling his forehead. "'Cause I never heard anything out of the ordinary from my hiding place."

"You never hear—or see—anything," I retorted, too weary to argue. What a disaster the Night of the Hairy Horror had turned out to be!

Everyone passed on going to the mall, so John dropped Kristen and me off at my house.

"Hey, talk to you later?" Sean called as I slammed the door. "I want to hear more about that big dog."

"Werewolf," I hissed through tight lips. "*Werewolf!*"

"Yeah, right, whatever," Sean said with a wink.

My mom and dad were waiting for us in the living room. Kristen ran over to hug my father and they chatted for a few minutes.

"I hope you like devil's food cake," my mom announced with a big smile, standing up. "I decided to bake Kristen an early birthday treat."

"Hey, great," Kristen said, then peered slyly at me. "Matt and I are going to need it after the crazy night we had."

My dad frowned. "Why, what happened?"

Kristen plopped into the rocking chair with an exaggerated sigh. "I'm too wiped to go into it. You tell them, Matt."

I ran a nervous finger across my upper lip. "Uh, I guess the werewolf double feature and then pizza at Roba's and everything made us both a little tired."

Kristen's lips twitched. "I was thinking something that happened *after* that. Remember, Matt?"

I shot my cousin a warning look. "I was thinking something that happened *before* the movies, having to do with the bridge railing. Does that ring any bells, Kristen?"

Two could play her game. There was a long, tense moment, and then Kristen jumped up.

"I'm ready for my cake, Aunt Val!"

I just bet you are, I thought smugly as we trooped into the kitchen. You can't have your little blackmailing cake and eat it too, Queen Bee. You squeal on me. I'll squeal on you.

I had a hard time falling asleep that night.

Kristen had taken over Chase's room, so my pesty brother moved in with me. Luckily his lengthy play date with Jason had tired him out, and he was sprawled on the air mattress, snoring, when I went to bed. Puddles curled up near my feet, his tail thumping against the covers. I felt safer with both my little brother and my dog close by. As much as I hated to admit it, my experience at the Singing Stones had thrown a real scare into me. Not only had I seen the town sign change earlier today, but I had heard those frightening growls inside the Palace Theater. And then to top it all off, I had halfheartedly tapped a stone under a full moon and heard it sing my name.

Seconds later the werewolf had appeared.

Coincidence? I didn't think so. Somehow I had awakened an evil force that was now roaming around Friendly Corners, really transforming it into Fiendly Corners. And if those other kids were telling the truth, the ones who had likewise witnessed spooky happenings, the force would soon be zeroing in on me.

Great, I thought nervously, scooting under the covers. I fell asleep that night, trying to remember everything I had seen in the movies or read in my horror stories about werewolves. I knew they were ordinary human beings who were cursed to change into wolves. Cursed to hunt for human flesh and blood when the moon was full. Dogs could detect the presence of werewolves, I sleepily realized. A silver bullet or silver weapon could stop them.

There was more, I thought, but I'd have to look it up.

Tomorrow, I decided. . . . After I returned to the Singing Stones to search for the cutout.

I drifted off, and dreamed about the Singing Stones. I pictured hitting the rock with the hammer and hearing it sing. The rock quivered, then ever so slowly was pushed aside. Long white skeletal arms reached out to me in the dark. A pale blur of a face stared greedily into my eyes, while a misshapen raw mouth opened: "*Matthewwww . . .*" It was a drawn-out whisper, like a sighing wind.

The cold white arms stretched up and again I heard the voice. . . .

I woke with a start, still hearing my name being called.

I lay frozen in bed, straining to listen. The wind whined along the crack of the windows, as if pleading to come in. It blew a shutter against a downstairs window.

The wind, I thought in trembly relief. Just the wind.

Over the rise and fall of that wind, however, I heard a long, wailing cry, faint and insistent.

"*Matthewwww. . .* "

It sounded sharper now, deeper, like wolves howling.

"Puddles?" I whispered, peering down the length of my bed. My dog was gone.

"Chase?" I said softly, ashamed to be calling my brother but overwhelmed by this throat-clenching fear. My brother snuffled in his sleep, and rolled over.

The light of the full moon poured through the bedroom window. It made eerie silver shadows in the dark. I threw off the covers and padded over to the window. Holding my breath, I peered down into our backyard. A black shape—a shadow of something?—melted into the bushes behind the garage.

I let out my breath in a terrified gasp and shrank back. Had the thing seen me?

There was a thump on the stairs, and Puddles burst into the room. He raced to the window, growling deep in his throat. Standing on hind legs, ears pricked back, he scratched and growled.

"What is it, boy?" I whispered, feeling a chill of dread come over me. "What's out there?"

Dogs detect the presence of werewolves, I remembered. They're their natural enemy.

Without warning Puddles turned and shot through the door, thumping his way down the stairs.

Would my dog try to attack whatever was out there?

Driven by a sense of urgency, I threw on a robe and slippers and hurried into the hallway. I stopped outside my parents' bedroom. Should I go and wake them up, tell them the Hairy Horror was watching our house? Yeah, right, I thought. Like they'd really believe a werewolf was loose in Friendly Corners.

I peered across at Chase's door. Should I wake Kristen? So far the Fearless Wonder had lived up to her name, but my pride wouldn't allow me to do it. My bragging cousin would never let me hear the end of it if I asked for her help.

I shook my head and accepted the inevitable.

I'd have to go downstairs by myself and stop Puddles from doing something foolhardy.

I gripped the belt of my robe in shaky fingers and tiptoed down the stairs.

"Puddles?" I whispered when I reached the hallway. "Come here. Now!"

The rooms were filled with shadows. The light of the moon coming through the living room window spotlighted the hanging planter by the sofa. The mass of leaves resembled a twitching nest of snakes. The rocking chair took on a menacing cast, a giant black beast waiting to pounce.

I swallowed nervously and whispered, "Puddles?"

I took a few hesitant steps toward the dining room when I heard a muffled thump. I stopped immediately, my head jerking back with the suddenness of the scare. My heart began pounding.

"Puddles?" I tried to call, but no words came out of my dry throat.

I could feel a pocket of cold air slide over my neck. A door or window must be open, I suddenly thought. At the exact moment I realized that, I heard something. The sound of breathing coming from the kitchen. Nails clicked on the linoleum. My heart lurched. My legs turned to rubber.

Something howled in the kitchen and was still.

Puddles, I thought in horror. The werewolf's attacking my dog!

Without hesitating, forgetting my fear, I raced into the kitchen.

Someone in the dark suddenly slammed the back door shut and then lunged directly at me!

CHAPTER TEN

I squealed in horrified shock and went crashing backward through the door.

I stumbled over my feet and tripped against the dining room table.

"Ouch!" I muttered, rubbing my sore shoulders and side.

The lights came on.

I jerked around to defend myself and found Kristen crouched in karate attack mode. Her arms were lifted and rigid. Her eyes were wild. She was wearing a long flannel granny nightgown decorated with ducks and oversized bunny slippers, but she still managed to look fierce.

"Matt!" she exclaimed, frowning and lowering her arms. "Why did you come barging into the kitchen like that? I thought you were a burglar!"

"That's nothing," I snorted. "I thought you were a werewolf."

"A werewolf? Oh, for pity's sake," Kristen groaned, "here we go again. Still trying to get to me with your horror stories."

"It's true," I said, rubbing my shoulders. "I saw something outside in the yard just now, and two guesses it's the Hairy Horror."

"The Hairy Horror, the Hairy Horror," Kristen said in a singsong voice. She wrinkled her stuck-up little nose.

"You lamebrain, you saw Puddles. He woke me up about ten minutes ago so I took him down here to let him out. That's what your werewolf is, your dog."

My mouth opened in shock. "You let Puddles out? After what we saw at the Singing Stones? You let my dog go out when there's a werewolf prowling around? Are you crazy?"

Kristen stared at me. "You're the nutcase, Matt. I think all this Fiendly Corners stuff has finally damaged some brain cells. Besides," she added, "he came right back in, took off for the stairs, then raced back to the kitchen only seconds ago. He howled once and I was just letting him out for the second time when you blew down the kitchen door."

I felt a sinking coldness in my stomach. Puddles was alone in the dark with that *thing*.

Pushing past my startled cousin, I hurried into the kitchen and stared out the windows over the sink.

Nothing stirred in the shadow-filled yard. Except for the wailing of the wind and the banging of the shutter against the side of the house, all was still.

Kristen joined me at the windows. "See?" she said, peering outside. "There's nothing there. No ghosts or werewolves from the Singing Stones. It's all in your mind."

"I know what I saw from my bedroom window," I said grimly. "And it wasn't Puddles."

I swallowed nervously and retied the belt of my robe.

I couldn't leave Puddles alone out there. I had to go and find him. And when I did, I hoped the Hairy Horror hadn't found him first.

"Wish me luck," I said in a falsely brave voice. I turned the knob of the back door and began to open it.

"Wait!" Kristen hissed.

71

I turned back, startled.

"You better arm yourself before you leave," my cousin said extra solemnly. Turning, she began to slide the drawers open near the sink. I watched in baffled silence as she fished through utensils, then triumphantly raised a fork. "It's not a silver bullet," she said, trying to hide a smirk, "but it should poke some holes in your big bad werewolf."

"Very funny," I said angrily. "I guess you're going to have to get an even closer look at the Hairy Horror to see that he's not some harmless big dog. But when you do, you won't be laughing. You and Sean both, you're in for a nasty surprise."

I yanked the fork out of her hand and threw it on the counter. Enough stalling, I told myself. It's time to hunt for Puddles. I reached out trembling fingers for the doorknob again and then stopped. Something inside me prevented me from turning it. I stood like a statue, motionless, too scared to complete this simple task.

"Oh, for pity's sake," Kristen burst out. "If you can't do it, I will."

She reached from behind me, grabbed the knob, and pulled the door open.

In the silver light of the full moon the Hairy Horror faced us, great fangs opened, dripping in anticipation.

It stood on its hind legs, all one hundred and fifty pounds of mean wolf, staring at us with hungry red eyes. Its lips were drawn back in an awful smile.

I let out a strangled cry of panic, stumbling against Kristen.

She gasped, clutching wordlessly at my shoulder.

No one blinked, no one breathed, no one moved.

We were suspended in a nightmare—until the werewolf reached out with one huge clawed paw.

"Quick, shut the door!" Kristen shouted. *"Shut the door!"*

We slammed the door hard on the creature, but were unable to close it completely. The werewolf snarled in pain and struck the wood with all his force. The door cracked open. A glistening black snout edged around the panel, pinkish tongue licking its lips. Demon-red eyes appeared and zeroed in on my terrified face. A hairy paw raked through the air, missing my hands by inches.

The werewolf threw back its head and howled, in hungry anticipation.

"Put more weight against the door!" Kristen cried.

I did as she commanded, but it wasn't working.

The force and power of the werewolf pushed the door open inch by terrifying inch. Another few inches and it would shove its way into the kitchen.

Kristen and I couldn't hold on. She was stronger than me, but we were both getting tired.

"What are we going to do?" I shouted.

The werewolf was snarling, enraged, slamming its weight against the flimsy barricade.

The repeated force of its blows made Kristen and me slide across the linoleum in our slippers. One more foot. . . . Six more inches . . .

The beast was so close I could feel its hot breath on my face.

A yellowed fang nipped close to my fingers.

"Don't let it bite or scratch you!" Kristen shrieked, slapping at its snout.

"If it bites you, you're a goner," I chanted hysterically under my breath. "If it bites you, you're a goner. If it bites you . . ."

Something golden brown and furry dashed through the opening in the door, between the werewolf's legs.

"Puddles!" I cried, grinning despite the awful circumstances. Puddles was alive. My dog hadn't been eaten.

In fact, Puddles wanted to devour the werewolf. He began snapping furiously at the creature's legs, growling savagely and barking.

"Puddles?" I whispered in shock. I had never seen my pet behave so ferociously before, but he was actually forcing the werewolf to back down. Puddles kept dancing close to the werewolf's legs, snapping and biting. The werewolf yelped, jumped back unexpectedly.

Kristen and I took advantage of the situation and slammed the door shut.

"Lock it!" I shouted. "Hurry!"

A second after Kristen turned the lock, the werewolf slammed its body against the door. It growled in frustrated rage and hunger.

"What are we going to do?" I asked Kristen.

She looked at me as if I weren't there. Her face was drawn and pale. She kept her fingers clenched around the lock and mutely shook her head.

I wanted to say, I told you so. See, there really is a werewolf.

But my cousin was in shock. The urge to needle her faded away.

Footsteps sounded on the stairs and my parents hurried into the kitchen.

"What in the world is going on down here?" my dad demanded sleepily. "I could hear you shouting and yelling all the way upstairs. Do you kids realize it's after one o'clock?"

My mom peered over at Puddles, who was yapping and scratching at the door.

"Why is he behaving so crazily?" she asked. "Does he want to go out?"

Kristen and I stared at each other in disbelief. The werewolf had been thudding against the door with such force that the wood was quivering. It had been howling loudly enough to wake the neighborhood. Yet in a matter of seconds, as if by magic, all was still. Had my parents— and the entire block—slept through the racket? Or were Kristen and I the only ones who could see and hear him?

"Werewolf," Kristen began babbling, pointing out the window.

"Werewolf?" my dad repeated, rubbing his bleary eyes. "Did I hear you say werewolf?"

My mom scowled at me. "Don't tell me you've been telling ghost stories to Kristen at this late hour. Werewolf, indeed. . . ."

I quickly glanced out the window. The animal was gone. The yard was deserted.

"Uh, she said *weird owl*," I corrected, throwing my cousin a warning glance. "Puddles must have spotted an owl in the dark and that's why he's so jumpy."

My dad yawned. "Owls in Friendly Corners? That's a first. Now if you two don't mind, your old man needs his beauty sleep. And get Puddles to quiet down, otherwise we'll have the neighbors complaining in the morning." He shook his head, flicked off the light, and murmured "owls" under his breath.

"Let's go, on the double," my mom commanded, herding Kristen and me back up the stairs. "We have a full day planned for you two tomorrow."

I stole a quick peek at Kristen.

She was shaking her head in a dazed manner, as if replaying the confrontation with the Hairy Horror.

Whatever my mom had planned for us would have to wait, I decided. Kristen and I had been singled out by a killer werewolf and the moon would be full again tomorrow night. That meant he'd come looking for us.

We needed to take action and find some answers.

And I knew the very person who could help us.

CHAPTER ELEVEN

Werewolves chased me all night long.

I thrashed around under the covers, dreaming of an entire pack of Hairy Horrors hot on my trail. They all had the same terrifying face, the rage-glowing eyes, the razor-sharp fangs that glistened in the moonlight. "*Matthew* . . ." they howled eerily, as they chased me through the woods. At times Kristen was running with me and at other times my dog. But we were never able to escape from the snarling pack.

Just as they were about to close in on me, I woke with a start. It was a bright and sunny Wednesday morning, and my heart and my legs were still pumping.

Something was pumping, but it was Puddles, lying on top of my bed and thumping away with his tail.

"Hey, boy," I whispered, reaching out to pet him. "That was some adventure we had. But you saved the day. You scared the werewolf away from the door."

"What werewolf?" Chase unexpectedly shouted in my ear. He hopped onto my bed and began jumping up and down on it. "You said werewolf. What werewolf?"

"Pipe down," I hissed, trying to grab his leg.

"Werewolf, werewolf, *werewolf!*" my brother cried in that piercing wake-up-the-whole-neighborhood voice.

"Listen, you little Rat-Face," I snarled, leaping up to tackle him. "Be quiet!"

"Mom!" he immediately screamed, kicking out at me. "Mom, Matt's hitting me again!"

"I am not," I retorted, but it was too late. My mom opened the door with a scowl on her face.

"Matthew Perry Walstrom," she commanded, "you let your brother go at once!"

"Wa-a-ahhh!" Chase cried, phonily rubbing away tears. "Matt punched and kicked me. He's always hitting me."

"Oh, brother," I muttered, releasing the pest. "I didn't hit him once. He was jumping up and down on my bed and saying stupid stuff."

Chase ran over to my mother and clutched at her leg. "Not stupid," he yelled, pointing at me. "You were talking about a werewolf and—"

"Werewolf?" my mom interrupted. She gave an exasperated sigh. "Not werewolves again, Matt. I thought we were finished with this last night. Are you telling your horror stories to Chase now as well as Kristen? You know I don't want you doing that."

"Uh, horror stories, right," I quickly agreed. "Stupid horror stories, that's all."

Chase shook his head indignantly. "No, that's not what Matt was saying. He said that Puddles saved the day by scaring the werewolf away from—uummmph!"

Suddenly a hand wrapped around my little brother's big mouth, cutting him off. Before he could react, Kristen leaned down next to him and whispered, "Wanna learn a good joke you can play on your friends? It has to do with potties." Luckily, Kristen had walked into the room just in time.

The little bug's eyes lit up. Kristen had said the magic word. Anything to do with bathroom humor got Chase's undivided attention.

"C'mon downstairs with me and I'll practice it with you," Kristen offered. She shot me a look before pulling the Rat-Face out of my bedroom. Saved by my cousin. Talk about a horror story growing stranger by the minute.

I hurriedly threw on my baggy jeans, an oversize flannel shirt and sneakers, and joined my family in the kitchen. Kristen was wearing another commando-type outfit and whispering in Chase's ear. He was listening with an earsplitting grin on his face. It must have been a terrific potty joke because he had completely forgotten about the werewolf. My mom and dad were dressed in jeans and sweatshirts, checking over a list that they put down as soon as I walked in.

"What's up?" I said, noticing how clean the normally messy kitchen table and countertops were.

"Glad you asked," my mom replied, holding up the sheet of paper. "This is a list of everything we have to do to prepare for Thanksgiving tomorrow."

"Not to mention Kristen's birthday," my dad added with a wink in my cousin's direction.

Kristen's thirteenth birthday. I had forgotten all about it in the wake of the Hairy Horror scare. The way things were going, I'd be happy if she and I survived another werewolf attack, let alone celebrated the day.

"Now the way I've got it figured out is this," my mom said. "There are chores for all of us to do to make it work. For starters, someone can help me bake the pies this afternoon and clean the good silver, while someone else can go into town with your father and do the grocery shopping."

"I want to help Kristen," Chase shouted, pulling at my cousin's hands.

I opened my mouth to protest, but slowly closed it again.

The most important thing I had to accomplish today wasn't polishing some old-fashioned silverware or helping my mom set the long dining room table. If there was going to be a full moon tonight I had to protect myself (and Kristen) by learning as much as I could about the Hairy Horror. And who knew better about the Romanian Gypsy curse than the person who worked on the movie set, Victor Cherkas?

Yesterday I would have turned and run in the opposite direction if Lizard Man Cherkas was heading my way. Today, however, was another story. Cherkas was the only person with knowledge of the werewolf curse. I had to take advantage of his offer to help that he'd made in the Palace Theater. And I had to do it before sundown if I knew what was good for me.

"I'll go with Dad to do the shopping," I quickly offered.

The least suspicious way to talk to Cherkas would be to run errands in the Square, then sneak off to the Riverside Inn for ten, fifteen minutes. I knew exactly what I'd say to my dad to gain that time: "I want to shop for Kristen's birthday gift." My dad was an old softie and he'd give me permission. It was a perfect plan and I was already mentally patting myself on the back when Kristen threw a wrench into it.

"No way, Matt," she announced. "I hate baking and cooking and I'd rather go grocery shopping than spend five minutes in a kitchen. You stay here and play chef."

I glared at her. "Too bad. I spoke up first. I'm going and that's final."

Kristen smiled sweetly at my dad. "It's my birthday week, Uncle Ken, so doesn't that mean I get my wish granted?"

I gritted my teeth. How could she be so bossy at a time like this? I thought fighting the werewolf together had changed her selfish little ways, but I was wrong. It would serve her right if the Hairy Horror poked his terrifying snout into her room tonight.

"If Kristen goes shopping, I want to go, too!" Chase cried. "I want to go. I want to go. I want to—"

"Quiet!" my soft-spoken mom suddenly shrilled, clapping her hands over her ears. "Give me some quiet to think."

While my mom conferred with my dad, I sidled up next to Kristen.

"Listen," I said in a soft voice, "I'm going to town to look up Victor Cherkas, so don't fight me on this. He knows all about the Hairy Horror."

She raised an eyebrow and stared at me for several drawn-out seconds. Then she nodded.

"We'll both go then."

"You're not going anywhere," I burst out, then reconsidered. If I kicked up a fuss, my parents would vote in favor of their darling little spoiled niece, and I'd be stuck at home. Besides, I thought in embarrassment, the Fearless Wonder wouldn't be a bad person to have with me in case anything unexpected should happen.

A half hour later the Bridal Path van was winging its way across the bridge. Normally I'd die first than be caught dead in the silver and pink wedding-cake decorated vehicle, but I had more important things to worry about. Kristen and I sat in the back, heads pressed together, whispering. I was telling her everything I remembered from the first meeting with Victor Cherkas.

"That's not a lot to go on," Kristen complained after I

finished. "He didn't give you any concrete facts about the Hairy Horror."

"Well, I know that," I retorted. "That's why we need to see him in person. Pump him for information about the curse. Maybe he can tell us how to remove it."

"He'd better," Kristen muttered. "I don't think I can stand a repeat performance of last night."

I nodded in worried agreement.

When the van approached the sign that hung over Main Street, Kristen and I peered intently at the shiny reflectorized letters.

I nudged her. "Friendly Corners," I said in relief. "The R didn't blink off."

"Does that mean the town's not haunted anymore and the werewolf won't bother us?"

"I don't know," I said, then made a funny, smothered sound. "Look at the word Friendly. It's changing! The R went out!"

Kristen peered at the sign through her bangs and went rigid. "*Fiendly Corners*," she said in a small voice.

"The town's still haunted," I said.

We looked at each other in alarm.

CHAPTER TWELVE

Kristen and I followed my dad around the Square, impatiently crossing off items from the shopping list. We bought gold and brown candles, paper turkey decorations, tiny pumpkins, specialty chocolates, and assorted nuts. Our last stop was the grocery store. When we had worked our way through half of the aisles, Kristen and I made our escape. My cousin asked to run to the Palace Theater to see if anyone found her lost cap, while I used the birthday gift excuse.

My dad grumbled, but good-naturedly gave in. "Make it short, though," he warned us. "No more than thirty minutes."

Kristen and I took off across the Square, backtracking to the Riverside Inn. Luckily for us the three-story white clapboard inn was situated right next to the bridge.

"Victor Cherkas?" Kristen asked the bored-looking clerk behind the registration desk. When he stared at us blankly she added, "He's expecting us."

"Room thirteen," the clerk said with a yawn. "It's all the way upstairs, top floor."

"Thirteen?" I said under my breath as Kristen and I began climbing the stairs. "That's a bad omen."

"Now you sound like your superstitious friend, Sean," she said, and froze as we reached the top floor. "Listen! Do you hear that?"

I bumped into Kristen, frowning. "What are we stopping for? I don't hear—"

Something growled. . . .

There was the sound of a scuffle, and then a piercing scream.

"Down the end of the hall," Kristen whispered. "Coming from room 13!"

Kristen darted down the hallway, but my feet refused to move. If the Hairy Horror was paying a visit to Victor Cherkas, I didn't want to see him again. My teeth began chattering. I tingled as if I'd stepped on a snake. All the while icicle insects marched up and down my spine.

Something snarled. . . .

I wanted to turn and run, but I couldn't. My cousin was standing outside room 13, ear pressed to the door. She turned and gestured to me.

I shook my head, indicating we should go.

"Chicken," Kristen muttered, and knocked on the door.

"Kristen," I croaked in a breathless voice. "No!"

A harsh cry came from the room, and another drawn out howl.

Kristen pounded on the door, calling out to Victor Cherkas.

With a little moan, I made myself run. As I reached Kristen, the door quivered, then burst open.

The Hairy Horror reared up like a monstrous cobra, demon-red eyes burning into our faces.

Kristen let out a muffled cry and bumped into me.

Help! I wordlessly screamed, pinwheeling my arms crazily for balance.

"Run!" Kristen shouted, shoving me from behind. "Go! Go! Go!"

Despite my panic I turned and glanced back.

A dark shape flew out of the room and came after us! "No!" I screamed.

A clawlike hand gripped my arm. I struggled and spun around.

Victor Cherkas was holding onto me, his lips twisted into a strange grin, his yellow eyes flickering with emotion. In his shiny black undertaker suit and dark tie, the wrinkled man resembled a thousand-year-old spider.

"Kristen, wait!" I shouted.

My cousin was racing down the stairs, lost to sight. As soon as I called out, however, she reversed and ran back up to the landing. She stood and stared at us with open mouth and bewildered eyes.

"Do not be scared," Victor Cherkas urged in his faint, but creepy voice. "I need to talk to you."

For such an old-looking guy, he had a surprisingly strong grip. I tried to wriggle free, but he held fast.

"We need to discuss the Hairy Horror," he said in a dry whisper.

I started, and he gave my arm a shake.

"I know," he hissed. "It is *alive*."

"But we just saw it in your room," I began to babble, "and we heard you scream. How come you weren't hurt?"

Cherkas jerked his head at the door and gave a humorless laugh. "Let me show you what you saw."

I hesitated, but Kristen set her jaw and marched straight up to the open door.

"Kristen, no!" I cried.

My cousin peered inside, then started. She gave a surprised snort.

"What?" I said when she pulled her head back out.

"What's going on? The Hairy Horror isn't in there?"

"Oh, it's there, all right," Kristen said. There was a strange expression on her face.

"Come," Cherkas gently prodded me. "You look."

On somewhat rubbery legs I inched over to the door, then jerked when I heard a ferocious howl.

"Go in and look," Cherkas repeated.

I screwed up my courage and did as he ordered. I got the shock of my life! The werewolf was most definitely present in the man's room, but in harmless cardboard form. Somehow the cut-out had managed to find its way back here.

I was about to ask Cherkas about that when I heard the sound of panting. The TV set was on in the far corner of the room, and a movie was playing. A monster movie, complete with howling dogs, angry mobs, and a gruesome-looking werewolf!

"My one obsession and area of study," Victor Cherkas murmured, indicating the screen. "All things having to do with lycanthropy—werewolfism."

I let out a relieved sigh. We had come to the right place then.

Kristen came up behind me and jabbed the cutout.

"What's going on?" she asked. "How did you get hold of this?"

Cherkas turned his gleaming reptile eyes on her. "And who might you be? A good friend of the boy, I assume?"

Wrong on two counts, I wanted to snap. I'm no *boy* and she's no *friend*.

"This is Kristen Powers, my cousin," I said. "She's staying with us over Thanksgiving."

"I am Victor Cherkas," the Lizard Man introduced himself, bowing slightly.

86

"I know, I mean, Matt's told me all about you," Kristen said, then loudly blurted, "what's going on? Why is the Hairy Horror chasing us? And what's it doing here in this cardboard form?"

Victor Cherkas held a bony finger to his lips as footsteps thudded down the hall. Someone tapped on the open door and the bored-looking desk clerk poked his head in.

"Sorry to disturb you," he said, "but we've received several complaints about the volume of your TV set. Could you lower it, please?"

If the blank-faced man noticed the Hairy Horror cutout, he didn't let on. He simply nodded at Victor Cherkas after delivering his monotone message, turned on his heel, and left.

"I don't wish to cause trouble," Victor Cherkas whispered with a strange smile. "I am here to prevent it. Come, let us take a walk outside."

I exchanged a glance with Kristen as the elderly man turned the set off, then took a heavy black coat out of the closet. Kristen held out her hands, palms up, and shrugged. Don't make waves, she seemed to be telling me. I nodded. We needed answers about the Hairy Horror and this ancient-looking reptile man was the only one who could help.

I didn't question him, therefore, when he picked up the cardboard cutout and offered it to Kristen. Their hands met, and Cherkas jumped, as if receiving an electric shock.

"Did my bracelet scratch you?" Kristen said, but Cherkas frowned, then brusquely motioned us out of the room.

When he turned to lock the door, I bent my head close to Kristen's.

"Just do what he says," I murmured, "no matter how strange."

Kristen rolled her eyes. "He *is* strange. And I get the creeps just holding this cutout. I don't want to be this close to the Hairy Horror, no matter how inanimate he is!"

"Let us walk outside by the river," Cherkas said in that raspy whisper.

We made our way down the stairs, Kristen keeping the cutout an arm's length from her body. No one was in the tiny lobby when we left. The clerk sat slumped over the front desk, eyes barely open.

We walked outside and followed Cherkas along the path that lead to the dock. It was chilly standing so near the river. Our breaths made frosty plumes in the air. Cherkas motioned for Kristen to put the cutout down and for us to draw closer. I mentally made a face, but did as he asked.

"Now I will tell you about the Hairy Horror," he whispered. His yellow eyes gleamed. "When I am done, you will know why I begged that Coffin man not to show the film or put this picture of the werewolf on display."

I shivered despite the warmth of the sun against our faces. A mass of icy air, drifting in from the water, seemed to drape itself around the three of us like an evil cobweb. Invisible strands of mist clung to our arms and legs, as if holding us prisoner. And all the while Victor Cherkas talked in that faint, but menacing voice.

Cherkas had worked as a special effects consultant on horror films, creating lifelike monsters for the string of hits directed by Wesley Graves in the '50s. But his greatest achievement was winning the position of special effects artist for the classic werewolf film of all time, *The Night of the Hairy Horror.*

Victor Cherkas rubbed his hands together as he paused in his story. "Now I will tell you something that no one else knows," he said in a dry whisper. "The only people who knew this incredible fact worked on the movie with me, more than thirty-five years ago. They are all dead, killed by the curse of the Hairy Horror. I am the only one left."

Kristen swallowed in the suspenseful silence that followed. My heart began pounding. We were about to hear the secret behind the Hairy Horror. I desperately wanted to know, yet I was afraid. My mouth felt dry and cottony.

Hoping I looked braver than I felt, I leaned forward and said, "What's the secret?"

Cherkas stared at Kristen and me for a long, breathless moment. His lizard tongue darted out and wet his dry lips.

"This goes no further," he warned us. "You must not tell a soul."

As if on cue, Kristen and I bobbed our heads.

"The man playing the part of the Hairy Horror was a Romanian Gypsy named Nicolae Padararu," Cherkas hissed, narrowing his eyes. "But he was no actor. He did not need my help with special effects. Do you understand what I am telling you?"

Kristen and I looked at each other. A horrified light dawn in both our eyes at the exact same time.

"You're telling us that the man, this Nicolae Gypsy, was a . . ." Kristen's voice trailed off.

"A *werewolf*," Victor Cherkas concluded with a cold, frightening smile.

CHAPTER THIRTEEN

Kristen and I stared unbelievingly at the old man.

My mouth opened and closed a few times before anything came out.

"But that's crazy!" I blurted. "There are no such things as . . ."

I peered across at the Hairy Horror cutout and stopped in midsentence.

Of course there were werewolves, I realized. One tried to attack Kristen and me just last night. A live version of the one standing on the dock with us, as a matter of fact.

Victor Cherkas leaned forward, eyes sweeping slowly over us as he spoke.

"Yes," he whispered, "you know I am speaking the truth. The director and his assistants captured Padararu one night while they were scouting locations in Romania. An old Gypsy woman, the boy's mother, pleaded and begged to have her son released, but they refused. When Padararu fell off a cliff into a river, she placed a horrible curse on the movie and all those who worked on it. The Spirit of the Hairy Horror would track us all down, one by one, and kill us."

Kristen edged nervously away from the cutout. "And the spirit is in this?"

Cherkas nodded and began to pace. "I have been following the whereabouts of the film and all its publicity stills and photos for over thirty-five years. Until this year they've been securely locked away in Monarch Pictures' vault. As soon as I learned *The Night of the Hairy Horror* was going to be released, however, I tracked down the location of the theater and came here immediately to warn your Commander Coffin."

"He didn't listen," I sighed, shaking my head.

"*You* didn't listen," Cherkas hissed angrily, wheeling about to face me. "You took the Horror up to the woods— oh, yes, I followed you, I knew you were involved in this because you heard the growls in the theater—and you exposed it to the full moon. The very worst thing you could have done."

"Well, I, ah, I didn't mean to—" I shrank under the poisonous stare of the old man. His eyes burned into mine with a ghostly yellow glow. "I'm sorry . . . "

"Saying you're sorry will not stop the Hairy Horror," Victor Cherkas rasped, one hand violently slashing the air. "*You* will be sorry if you do not heed my words. Time is short. There will be a full moon again this evening. The werewolf will seek you out, he *must* seek you out, to ful-fill the ancient curse."

"But why Matt?" Kristen broke in with a puzzled frown. "I thought he'd go after you since you worked on the picture."

Cherkas pushed his cobwebby hair out of his eyes to focus on her. "The boy took the Horror to the woods and exposed him to the moonlight. He chanted something—I do not know what he said, I was too far away. Whatever it was, the werewolf was awakened. And his next victim will be Matt. Unless . . . "

"Unless *what*?" I cried, sensing a glimmer of hope. "Is there a way to stop him?"

"Tell us!" Kristen demanded, green eyes flashing. "Please help us!"

Cherkas frowned thoughtfully and pointed to the cutout. "There is a test we can perform right now to find out if the werewolf will come after the boy. Werewolves detest water. They will not cross a body of water if they can help it. If Matt throws the cutout into the river, and it sinks, he is safe. The spirit has been drowned."

"Why couldn't someone have tried to sink it before?" Kristen asked with a puzzled frown. "The werewolf would have been killed years ago."

"The cutout was locked away before I could get to it," Cherkas explained. "No one was allowed into Monarch's vaults. And only the next intended victim of the Horror can perform this task."

"And that's Matt," Kristen said in a hushed voice. She handed me the cutout.

I hesitated. "It belongs to Commander Coffin. I promised him I'd return it."

"Oh, for pity's sake," Kristen burst out, "you'd rather be eaten alive by a werewolf than break a promise to Commander Coffin? Are you nuts?"

"I will reimburse Commander Coffin for the loss of his cutout," Cherkas informed me. "*If* the Horror sinks, that is."

I nervously shuffled my feet. "What if it doesn't?" I said feebly.

His reptile eyes blinked at me. His lips drew back in a grimace.

"If the Horror floats, then we know the spirit is truly alive and will be returning tonight. And we will then discuss our second course of action."

"And that is . . . ?" Kristen asked.

"Returning to the exact spot where the Horror was awakened and facing it directly."

My mouth flopped open. Even Kristen looked stunned.

"Go back to the Stones after dark and wait for the werewolf to come get me?" I said in a high-pitched squeak. "I don't like that plan. I don't like that plan at all!"

"It is the only way to confront the Hairy Horror and trap him," Cherkas urged me. "I will be there, as well. I will bring certain items to destroy the creature. You will be safe, never fear."

"I *do* fear," I protested. "I fear very much."

Cherkas nodded at the cutout. "Perhaps we will not need to return to the woods. The water could destroy the Horror."

Kristen dug her nails into my arm. "Do it, Matt! Throw it into the water!"

What choice did I have? I was all set to pick up the cutout when a black Doberman shot along the path and came to a screeching halt at the foot of the dock. Panting and snarling, the animal paced about twenty yards from us.

Victor Cherkas took a clumsy step back and bumped into the cutout.

"It senses the werewolf," he hissed in a terrified voice. "Matt, toss the Horror into the river. Do it now!"

My suddenly rubbery fingers clutched at the cutout as the Doberman growled menacingly. The dog pulled its lips back to bare its sharp teeth.

"Matt, throw the Horror into the water," Cherkas pleaded.

"What if the dog comes after me if I do?" I whispered.

"It doesn't want you, it wants the Hairy Horror," Kristen shouted.

She gave my arm a shove and I skidded on the wet dock. The Doberman growled threateningly as I squeaked and lost my balance. Clutching the cutout to my chest, I stumbled off the dock—

And plunged feetfirst into the icy water of the river!

CHAPTER FOURTEEN

Inky blackness enveloped me. The cutout was wrenched out of my hands by the current. Holding my breath I kicked my arms and legs, trying to break through to the surface. My legs touched on something—a rocky ledge?—and I poked my head out of the water. Kristen's worried face peered down at me from the edge of the dock. Another face, one I didn't recognize, stared at me, too.

"Matt," Kristen was shouting, "grab hold of this man's hand!"

The stranger, a big, burly man with a reddish beard and ski jacket, crouched on the dock and extended his arm to me. Behind him the Doberman was panting and eyeballing me, body rigid.

I doggy paddled four feet or so to cling to the side of the dock. The man leaned down and yelled, "Take my hand! I'll help pull you out."

I thrashed helplessly in the water, staring into the black marble eyes of the Doberman.

As if sensing my fear, the man whistled to the dog and it promptly sat.

"Roger won't hurt you," the man assured me. "He's as harmless as a baby."

Right, I thought. You should have seen your *baby* two minutes ago when it was in killer attack mode.

"Come on!" the man prompted me. "Grab my hand."

Grunting in effort, I reached out and touched the stranger's hand. Immediately iron strong fingers closed over my wrist and pulled me out of the river. I flopped onto the dock like a beached whale, drained, wet, and cold. Water streamed out of my clothes and sneakers. My hair was plastered all over my face.

Kristen dropped to her knees beside me. "Matt, are you all right?"

I rolled over and sat up, peering at her from water-spiked eyelashes.

"I'm fine," I said almost testily, and then looked up at the man. "Hey, I owe you a big thanks."

"It's okay," the man said with a smile, then scratched his beard. "I still can't figure out why you'd take a dive into the river on a cold day like this."

"I didn't mean to," I said. "It was an accident. I'd never deliberately—"

I paused for a moment, gazed wildly around.

"Hey!" I cried. "Where's Victor Cherkas? What happened to him? And Kristen, what happened to the cutout?"

I jumped to my feet, ignoring my chattering teeth and waterlogged condition. In the excitement of the last few minutes, I had completely forgotten about the Hairy Horror and my all-important test. I stared across the water, searching for the cutout. Hoping it would not be seen. Praying it had sunk.

Kristen gave a funny little cough. Not in front of this man, she seemed to be warning me.

"Well, if you two don't need me anymore," the man said, "I'll be on my way." He peered at me with a worried smile. "If I were you, buddy, I'd go right home and change into warm clothes. No more swimming lessons for you today."

I shot him a nervous grin and watched as he and his dog walked back along the path to the front of the inn. As soon as he was gone I wheeled around to face Kristen.

"What happened after I fell?" I demanded impatiently.

Kristen rolled her eyes. "It was pretty unbelievable. You went into the river and I grabbed at that creepy Cherkas character to get him to help me pull you out. He practically frothed at the mouth, shook off my hand as if I had cooties, and tripped over himself to get to the cutout."

My mouth dropped open. "The cutout? You mean the cutout didn't sink?"

"It bobbed right back up as soon as you released it," Kristen replied unhappily. "And that Cherkas ignored *you* to fish it out. As soon as he got his hands on it, he turned to me and whispered, 'I'll be contacting you later,' and then split." She snorted. "The Doberman started following him, but that's when the owner showed up and called his dog off. And the rest, as they say, is history."

"So Cherkas has the cutout," I said in a tense voice. I peered nervously at Kristen. "Does that mean we have to go to the Stones tonight?"

She threw up her hands. "I don't know. I don't know any more than you do. But I do know this." She pointed to her watch. "If we don't get back to the grocery store to meet your dad, we're going to be in big trouble."

I stared down at myself. "I can't go back looking like this! I'll be grounded for a month. Forget a month. A year! What am I going to tell my dad?"

Kristen's lips twitched. "Let me handle it. I'm a pro when it comes to getting myself out of trouble, and boy, do I ever get in trouble."

"Yeah, but I don't like lying to my parents," I said glumly, following my cousin along the path that led to the bridge. "Maybe I fudge a little, or omit certain facts, but I try not to lie about the big stuff."

"So tell them the truth," Kristen snapped. "See if you don't get grounded anyway for spreading stupid were-wolf stories. You think they're going to believe that the Hairy Horror is after you because you awakened its spirit at the Singing Stones?"

I stared at her a long moment, then shook my head with a sigh.

"You just leave this to me," she said.

She was right. I wanted to tell my parents about the trouble I was in, but I knew they wouldn't believe me. It would make matters worse if I did get grounded. The Hairy Horror would come to our house tonight, and this time the entire family would be threatened. I didn't want that to happen. I'd have to screw up my courage and return to the Stones to destroy the werewolf once and for all. Besides, I'd have the Lizard Man and the Fearless Wonder for back up. I wouldn't be alone.

Kristen and I trotted along the walkway of the bridge, then stopped for the light on Main Street.

Todd Slivack rode by on a bike, followed by two of his peanut-butter-brained friends.

"Hey, Matty," he called when he spotted me. "You look positively . . . "

He paused when Kristen stepped forward.

"Soggy," he finished lamely.

Guffawing, the trio rode off.

"I'd like to sic the Hairy Horror on *them*," I growled.

Kristen laughed, then nudged me forward when the light turned green.

Nobody was laughing when we caught sight of my dad a minute later. He was standing outside of the grocery store, arms crossed in front of his chest, a scowl on his face. The scowl deepened when he saw my watery condition.

"What in the world happened to you?" he angrily demanded. "You're both ten minutes late, and I was beginning to get worried. Now you show up soaking wet in the middle of winter!"

"I can explain," I nervously began.

"Oh, boy, you better," my dad snapped. "But let's hear it inside the van. It's too cold to stand around talking in your state."

I threw an alarmed glance at Kristen as we scrambled into the van and my dad turned on the heater. She gave me a reassuring smile.

"Listen, Uncle Ken, this is all my fault," she stated, making her voice all trembly and soft. "It all started when Matt and I were leaving the grocery store together and this black dog, a Doberman, I think, started scaring me."

My dad started the car and peered at her in the rearview mirror. "A Doberman?"

Kristen's bottom lip quivered. "It was awful. It started barking at me and I got scared. I took off and ran. I ran to get away from the dog and I ended up down by the bridge. Matt followed me, to make sure I was all right."

The scowl had left my dad's face. "Go on," he said.

"I still heard it behind me and I ran down to the bank, and that's when I dropped my glove. It fell into the river."

I stared down at Kristen's hands, both encased in gloves. I poked her and made a face. She hurriedly peeled one off and stuffed it in a pocket of her jacket.

"Then what happened?" my dad asked in a sympathetic voice.

"I tried to lean over to grab my glove, but Matt said he'd get it for me, and I said, no! but he insisted. That's when he lost his balance and fell in."

I couldn't believe it. Kristen had turned a potentially ugly situation for me into a positive one. My dad was actually peering at me with a proud twinkle in his eye.

"You both shouldn't have gone near the water," he said, "but I guess Matt meant well."

"Oh, he did," Kristen gushed.

I kicked her leg. *Don't overdo it*, I tried to warn her.

But my dad had bought my cousin's outrageous story. Talk about fairy tales!

"I think my son deserves a special treat for his good deed," my dad pronounced. "Matt, can you think of something?"

"Uh, I'll tell you later if I come up with anything," I mumbled. I shrank back against the seat, feeling my cheeks flush in embarrassment. I would be so happy once this business about the Hairy Horror was over.

"I can't believe I missed all this!" Sean groaned. He slammed the basketball against the cement driveway and stared at Kristen and me. "Why do I always miss out on all the good stuff?"

I reached up and patted his shoulder. "It's your destiny, I guess. In your horoscope, you know?"

"Not funny, Walstrom," Sean protested.

Sean, Kristen, and I were out in our backyard, tossing a basketball at the hoop over our garage. Kristen and I had spent the rest of the morning helping my mom around the house, vacuuming, polishing silver. Kristen had taken a few too many breaks, but because it was her birthday week, she got away with it. After lunch we had called Sean over to shoot baskets. Naturally, we had filled him in on what had happened with Victor Cherkas and the Hairy Horror cutout, not to mention the werewolf attack from the night before.

"I'm cursed," Sean whined, after failing to dunk a basket. "Not just in basketball, but in life. How come I never get to see a real werewolf?!"

"Hey, you really want to see the Hairy Horror?" I asked him. "You wait until tonight. You'll see the Hairy Horror and wish you hadn't."

"It was that scary?" Sean whispered, his eyes round. "As scary as in the movies?"

"Worse," I replied, unable to repress a shudder. "*Much* worse."

"I've been reading up on werewolves from your collection of horror books," Kristen said. She came up behind me and stole the ball away.

"No fair!" I angrily shouted, and watched my show-off cousin sink yet another basket. She turned and hurled the ball at Sean who caught it with a grunt.

"There's something strange going on," Kristen said. She scrunched up her forehead. "I didn't have that much time to research, but some things don't add up."

"*Nothing* adds up about this Hairy Horror curse," I said. I wheeled around and tried to take the ball out of Sean's hands, but he dribbled it out of reach. "The whole thing doesn't make sense."

"No, I mean things I've been reading about werewolves and what Victor Cherkas told us."

"Yeah, but he's an expert on the subject," I said. "I'd trust his word over something in a book."

"But he acted so oddly this morning," Kristen said. There was a thoughtful look in her eyes. "I can't quite put my finger on it, but something's been bothering me."

"We haven't heard anything from either Commander Coffin or Cherkas, so maybe he returned the cutout to the theater and that'll be the end of it," I said.

"Wishful thinking," Kristen said. She tore across the driveway to intercept Sean when Chase poked his head out of the back door.

"Matt, telephone!" he shouted. He began jumping up and down to impress Kristen. "Come in quick!"

"Who is it?" I asked, not wanting to stop playing.

"Someone named Turkey," he giggled in a high-pitched voice. "Jerky Turkey!"

"Go back inside, Rat-Face," I shouted in annoyance. "Quit bugging me with your lamebrain jokes."

"It's no joke," he exploded. "It's Turkey. Victor Turkey."

"*Cherkas*," Kristen said in a whisper.

Victor Cherkas. This couldn't be good news.

A shiver prickled down my back.

I threw an uncertain glance over my shoulder as I walked into the house with draggy footsteps.

CHAPTER FIFTEEN

"Are you feeling all right?" my mom said, getting up from the dining room table. She came over and placed a hand on my forehead.

"I'm fine," I snapped, staring down at my plate. "I mean, jeez, Mom, that's the fifth time you've asked me that tonight."

She looked at me with concern. "You've hardly touched your dinner. And you didn't even have dessert, and I know my home-baked chocolate chip cookies are your favorite."

"I-I'm not hungry, I guess," I mumbled.

"I can eat Matt's cookies for him," Chase announced. He thrust a greedy hand at the cookie plate, knocking over his glass of milk.

"Oh, honey," my mom sighed, running into the kitchen for paper towels.

"Way to go, squirt," I said.

But I was happy for the interruption. All during dinner my mom had been staring at me, studying my face for signs of fever or chills. My dad had given her the falling-into-the-river-to-save-Kristen's-glove story when we got home and she had been hovering over me all day.

Yes, I probably did look pale and glassy-eyed, but it had nothing to do with my icy plunge in the river. I kept thinking about the conversation I had with Victor

Cherkas, replaying it in my mind. "You *must* come to the woods tonight at eight o'clock, the same spot where you awakened the werewolf," he commanded me. "I will bring the cutout and other items necessary to destroy the Hairy Horror."

"But can't I just stay at home, lock the door, and hide?" I had replied. "Tomorrow the full moon will be gone and I'll be safe." "Until the next full moon, or the one after that," Cherkas had hissed. "The Horror will not give up until he gets to you, or to your family."

That decided me. I promised to return to the Singing Stones at eight o'clock and hung up. I may have agreed to be there, but I didn't have to like it.

Like it? I was scared to death.

At least I had support, however. Kristen had insisted upon going back with me, as did Sean. "I'm not missing my one chance to see a real, live werewolf!" he had said. Sean wouldn't be feeling so brave once he got close to the Hairy Horror, but I didn't want to exclude him from our adventure. It was all set. I had asked my parents if Kristen and I could run across the street at seven-thirty to watch rented videos with Sean, and they had agreed. Sean had asked his parents if he could come over to our house for the same reason.

We left our respective houses at seven-thirty sharp and met behind Sean's house. I brought my bike with me, while Sean would take his and Kristen would use John's old bike. It was a cold, cloudy night, but the full moon would peek through every so often. In accordance with the weather Kristen and I had dressed extra warmly.

"Lots of padding in case of emergency," Kristen said with a laugh, but her usual smirk was strained. In this case emergency could mean werewolf fangs or claws.

We rolled out the two bikes from the O'Shea garage and talked in whispers.

"What's with the backpack?" Sean asked Kristen. "You look like you've got a bowling ball in there!"

"She's not telling," I said. "I already asked her. It's some big secret."

"No big secret," Kristen replied defensively. "I want to have a few tricks up my sleeve in case Creep Man Cherkas makes any mistakes."

I frowned at her. "He's a werewolf expert. I trust him. If it weren't for Cherkas, I probably wouldn't even be here right now. He's helping us, Kristen, so don't get on his case."

Sean peered at his illuminated watch. "We better get moving if we're going to get to the Stones by eight. Before we go, though, I wondered if you wanted to hear what my horoscope predicted for tonight?"

Kristen and I looked at each other. "NO," we both said in unison.

"Hey, thanks a lot," Sean said in a hurt voice.

"Read it to us *after* we demolish the werewolf," Kristen suggested and winked at me.

If, I nervously wanted to correct her. *If* we demolish the werewolf. But I kept silent. No need to infect anyone else with this chilling premonition of fear. Oh sure, I had been antsy all afternoon just like Kristen, wondering what would happen tonight at the Stones. But I trusted Victor Cherkas. I was ninety-nine percent certain he'd squash the curse of the Hairy Horror and I'd be fine. It was that awful one percent of uncertainty I worried about. And as we began pedaling down the street, I was suddenly overcome by this powerful feeling of dread. An icicle cold finger tickled the bumps down my spine, warning me not to go to the Stones. *Turn back*, it told me.

But I couldn't.

I changed gears and pedaled harder, trying to keep up with my friends.

It took us fifteen minutes of heavy duty uphill pedaling to reach the turnoff for the Stones. No one talked the entire time. We swung into the bumpy narrow lane and suddenly the trees closed in around us. The noise and sounds of town might never have existed. We were cut off completely, alone in a place of chilly darkness and squirming shadows. As we pedaled nearer to the entrance, the air seemed to change around us. It had been crisp and cold, but now a thin mist seeped damply into the necks of our jackets. I shivered and pedaled harder.

Sean pulled up next to me. "Where's this Cherkas guy meeting us?"

"He didn't say. Probably inside the clearing, where I hit the stone."

Kristen zoomed out in front. "Does he know you're bringing us?"

I blinked, trying to remember. Had I mentioned Sean and Kristen in the conversation?

I shook my head slowly. "I don't know. I don't think so. But it's pretty unlikely I'd come all the way up here alone. No way!"

"Fine," Kristen said. "You brought Sean with you for moral support, that's all. I'm invisible from here on in."

We rode along the shoulder of the road and pulled up by the chained entrance. After we quietly hid the bikes behind some bushes, I confronted my cousin.

"What are you talking about?" I said in a tense whisper. "You're not going anywhere alone. It's too dangerous."

"I can take care of myself, in case you haven't

noticed," Kristen retorted. "Just trust me on this. It's safer for everybody if we split up."

I started to argue with her when we heard a sound.

A branch snapped somewhere in the woods.

"Listen!" Kristen said in a whisper.

We peered all around us, trying to figure out the cause of the sound.

Another branch snapped. The woods creaked secretively. I looked up, noticing how two large branches in a tree rubbed together in the wind.

I let out a shaky laugh and pointed. "It's that tree, see? Just branches creaking together."

"Branches," Sean repeated with that dorky chuckle. "I knew that."

I fumbled in my pocket and pulled out a tiny flashlight. "Now that we've finished scaring ourselves to death, it's time to go in. Everybody ready?"

I stared at their faces in the moonlight. Sean took a big gulp, and nodded. Kristen started to say something, but changed her mind.

"Ready," she whispered. There was a determined glint in her eye.

I grabbed her arm. "Promise me, Kristen. Promise you won't do anything, well, stupid."

She smiled grimly. "I promise."

"Let's go then."

We scooted beneath the chain and paused just inside. Overhead clouds cruised across the moon. Total darkness engulfed us. The leafless trees that formed a canopy over our heads turned into black skeletons, their twisted limbs clawing at the sky. Shadows slithered and squirmed along the path.

I peered into the woods, half afraid of what I might see.

The darkness seemed to come alive at that moment. Something in the woods took a deep breath, and exhaled.

"Did you hear that?" I said in a shaky voice.

"What?" Sean mumbled.

A howl, long and drawn out, pierced the absolute stillness.

"Behind us!" Sean shrieked, poking me in the back.

Terror as hot as an iron clamped onto my chest.

"Run!" I shouted. "*Run!*"

I forgot about the flashlight in my panic. We took off in the direction of the Stones, lurching and stumbling and gasping for breath. My heart thudded uncontrollably in my chest. My hands had turned to ice.

We rounded a curve and came upon the clearing.

The moon peeked out from behind its curtain of clouds. A shaft of silvery light spilled across the jagged rocks and boulders.

I began scrambling over the tombstone-shaped slabs, trying to find the spot where the spirits "sang" to me.

"We'll be safe here!" I cried. "The werewolf didn't attack us when we were in the Stones, so maybe we'll be protected."

"Man, that was close," Sean blurted, crawling over the rocks and boulders behind me.

"Kristen, are you all right?" I shouted.

There was a long tense silence.

"Kristen?"

I stopped, glancing over my shoulder.

Kristen was gone. She had vanished into the woods and was nowhere to be seen.

CHAPTER SIXTEEN

A sick feeling slid into my stomach.

"Where did she go?" Sean exclaimed. "What happened to her?"

"I don't know." I stared into Sean's frightened face with a sense of dread. "Could the werewolf . . . ? I mean, did she run into the Hairy Horror on the path and then . . ."

I remembered the incredible strength of the creature and the razor-sharp fangs in its mouth, and my voice trailed off. I shuddered.

"We've got to go look for her," I said. "Right now!"

"Right," Sean agreed, but his voice came out in a squeak.

"You wanted to see a werewolf," I reminded him, "and now's your chance."

He grimaced as we began stumbling and crawling back over the rocks.

"*Mat-the-e-e-w* . . ." a voice suddenly whispered. "*Matthew . . .*"

I stopped, jerking my head around.

"Matthew, over here."

The whisper was deep, almost a growl. I peered into the edge of the clearing and thought I saw a dim shape. A shape moving between the dark trees. The mist rising from the stones blurred my vision. I squinted and saw the shape edging its way to the clearing.

"Who is it?" Sean whispered, clutching at my arm.

"I can't be sure," I said.

The shape had been a blur before, a dark spot floating among the shadows. But now it took on definition. It was a man, of medium height and solidly built, draped completely in black. Only a pale blur of a face appeared beneath some kind of hood.

"Matthew, you must come *now*," the gravelly voice hissed.

"Mr. Cherkas?" I called. "Is that you?"

An arm appeared and motioned to me.

"At once," the voice commanded. "The werewolf is on its way!"

"We heard it!" I exclaimed. "Behind us on the path. And now Kristen is gone. You have to help us find her."

The figure of Victor Cherkas inched a few feet closer to the clearing. The silvery gleam of the full moon was half obscured by those clouds again. Try as I might, I couldn't get a good look at the old man's face. It was a round white blur, an eerie Halloween mask of dark eyes and shadowy features.

"Mr. Cherkas?" I repeated. "Did you hear me? My cousin's missing and we need your help."

He held up a hand. "She is in no danger. *You*, however, will be attacked if you do not join me in the woods."

I experienced a sharp prick of alarm.

The Hairy Horror was coming.

"I'll go with you," Sean offered as I began scrabbling over the fifty feet or so of upturned rocks and boulders.

Cherkas's voice rang out like a whip. "He joins me—alone."

Sean and I stopped, and stared at each other, but I finally nodded my head. "Gotta do what he says. He's the werewolf expert."

"Yeah, but—"

"You want to help?" I said. "Go look for Kristen."

Brave words, sending Sean off while I had to remain to face the Hairy Horror, but I was feeling anything but brave. That overwhelming feeling of dread, of fear, had come back, stronger than before. It crashed through me like an evil tidal wave. And just like being under water, I couldn't breathe, I couldn't swallow, and now, unfortunately, I couldn't seem to move.

I watched Sean scramble away from me in a fit of panic. Another few feet and he was gone, swallowed up by the trees. I was completely alone.

"It is time, Matthew," Cherkas growled. Funny how his dry little whisper voice had gotten deeper. And funny, also, that he seemed to have gotten taller—bigger—since I last saw him this morning. Granted he was covered up from head to toe in some hooded getup, but the shrunken little lizard that I remembered had altered in some mysterious way.

"I'm coming," I said, forcing myself to climb over the rocky terrain.

My hands were slippery with sweat. It made scrambling crablike over the stones more difficult. My legs felt wooden and uncoordinated, like a puppet's. My breath came in ragged gasps. The closer I approached the edge of the clearing, the more my body resisted. It was almost as if my gut knew something my brain didn't.

"Weird stuff," I said under my breath. "Now I sound like Sean." I laughed, but the smile faded when I caught a glimpse of something lurking behind Victor Cherkas.

111

I froze immediately, making a tiny, stifled choking sound.

"Do not be afraid," Cherkas ordered in that quavery rumble. He held out his hand. "I have Romanian herbs and other objects to break the curse."

It was now or never. Taking a deep breath, I got ready to jump off the last flat rock when a twig snapped like a tiny explosion.

An all-too-familiar figure slid out from behind Cherkas. Kristen had been lurking behind him!

"Don't do it, Matt!" Kristen shouted. "Don't do anything he says!"

CHAPTER SEVENTEEN

There was a moment of stunned silence.

I stared at Kristen in a kind of stupefied shock—and embarrassment.

"Don't take another step," she ordered me. "Stay inside the Singing Stones."

"But Mr. Cherkas is going to help me," I cried. "He's the only one who can stop the werewolf from attacking."

Cherkas bared his teeth in more of a snarl than a smile. "Do not listen to the girl," he demanded. "The Hairy Horror is coming, and you will be destroyed out there in the open. I can protect and shield you," he continued. "I can destroy the monster before he destroys you."

"Lies," Kristen snapped. "All lies. And I can prove it."

"Kristen," I began, trying to reason with her, motioning for her to listen. "Mr. Cherkas knows what he's doing. He's trying to help—"

Her face was pale, but a kind of stubborn anger blazed in her eyes. When I took a step forward, she threw out her hands as if to push me back.

"I'm warning you, Matt," she cried, "stay right where you are!"

"The girl is deluded," Victor Cherkas rasped, a trace of scorn in his voice. "If you listen, you will be killed. Yes, *killed*," he emphasized, seeing my eyes bug out.

"Kristen, I have to," I whispered. "I have to!"

My cousin dug frantically in her backpack and produced something that resembled a gun.

"And if I have to, I'll use this," she threatened, waving the weapon high.

I let out a terrified squeak, then realized it was my little brother's Super Soaker.

"A squirt gun?" I blurted.

Had she totally lost it?

But Victor Cherkas was no longer eying her with contempt. Something flickered in those yellow eyes. Uncertainty, maybe? Or nervousness?

Why should he be nervous about a stupid squirt gun?

"Put that foolishness away," he ordered. "Of what use is a child's toy against a werewolf?"

Kristen jerked her arm around, training the Super Soaker on him.

"Just hear me out," she said in a trembling but defiant voice.

"There is no time," Cherkas growled. "The Horror is almost upon us. And we are not prepared. Matt is not prepared."

"Lie number one," Kristen said angrily. "The Hairy Horror *isn't* out there, about to pounce. The Hairy Horror isn't hidden in the woods at all."

"Wha-at?" I gasped. My mouth opened and closed in shock. "What do you mean?"

"I mean," Kristen retorted, "that the Horror isn't lying in wait for you, Matt. The Hairy Horror is standing in front of us—*at this very minute!*"

I shook my head hard, as if trying to shake some sense out of her crazy statement.

"You don't mean. . . . You're not really saying—" I

stammered, swiveling my head to look at Victor Cherkas.

"Ridiculous," the old man pronounced, throwing up his hands.

The moon slid completely free of the clouds, illuminating the clearing with brilliant radiance. I stared at the hands extended to me, and took an instinctive step back. The palms were slightly hairy, the nails long and curved.

Wolf paws!

I let out a gasp, my heart racing double-time.

"But I-I don't understand," I said aloud. "I don't get it."

Victor Cherkas made a sudden swipe of that horrible paw/hand in my direction, but Kristen shot a stream of water at him. The water hit his palm with a sizzle. Cherkas shrieked, snarling in pain and outrage.

"Don't make another move," Kristen threatened him. "I'll get you in the face if you do."

At any other time I would have been laughing, watching my cousin hold someone captive with a squirt gun. I wasn't laughing now. I was too terrified. If what she said were true, then the Hairy Horror would spring out of his disguise at any moment and easily rip my throat apart.

The person (monster!) we called Cherkas suddenly opened his mouth in a snarl. The silvery glow of the full moon flashed against his teeth. Even as we watched in panicked silence, the ancient-looking molars and incisors were lengthening into needlelike fangs, pointed and deadly. The nose shifted, spreading like melting wax into a glistening black snout. And the once-yellow eyes, now furnace red, burned into mine with hate-filled fury.

"Kristen . . ." I moaned, wanting to turn and run, but unable to tear my gaze from those eyes.

Hungry eyes.

115

Bottomless eyes.

A person could get lost in those flaming red depths.

And then, incredibly, the snout opened. "It is your turn now," a half human, doglike voice growled. "The Horror attacked and bit me last night in these woods. He disappeared and I became the werewolf. Now I must pass on the curse to you."

Kristen and I stared helplessly as the black-hooded figure of Victor Cherkas began to sink down, rippling in the moonlight. A hideous furred paw reached up and ripped the hood away, so that the full moon could shine directly on his head. At first it seemed as if he were merely sitting down, but then his body began twisting and writhing, and his black coat with it. His shrunken chest broadened and lengthened. His shoulders hunched. He tore his coat and clothes away with his fangs so that his gigantic wolf's body could be set free.

Watching us with glittering eyes and an awful smile, he crouched on his haunches.

"Kristen?" I managed to croak.

"Here," she shouted, "take the gun!"

Before I could react, she lobbed the Super Soaker at me. It fell just short of the Stones.

"Pick it up!" she screamed, while digging frantically in her backpack. "Get it, Matt!"

I hesitated, and in that moment, the werewolf was on his feet. Forcing myself to move, I jumped across the short distance between the clearing and the woods and bent to grab the squirt gun.

The Horror howled in anticipation and leapt at me, teeth bared.

I ducked and rolled at the last minute, snatching the squirt gun.

116

The werewolf growled in frustration, spun around, and charged.

Without pausing to think, I shot a full dose of water squarely in his face.

Direct hit! With a screaming snarl he was thrown ten feet away and landed heavily on his side. A reddish vapor rose from his fur. Apparently stunned he lay there among the trees, motionless.

"Come on!" Kristen shouted. She gave my arm a hard shove and pushed me away from the werewolf. Into the darkness of the woods.

"But—shouldn't we head toward the Stones?" I cried, skidding to a stop.

She grabbed my hand and tugged me after her. I couldn't resist. She was stronger and faster and bigger than me.

"I found something earlier that can help us in here," she whispered. "But we've got to hurry. He'll be after us soon!"

I couldn't catch my breath. We slapped our way through branches and bushes, never once pausing to look back.

"Hurry!" Kristen kept chanting. "Hurry!" She was an out-of-control locomotive engine and I was the helpless caboose.

I felt her panic. It worsened when we heard the unmistakable sound of something crashing after us in the underbrush. The werewolf was gaining. He was so close we could hear his panting and his snarls.

"He's catching up to us!" I shouted.

CHAPTER EIGHTEEN

I swung my head around and screamed. He came after us on all fours, his mouth open in rage, his fangs exposed. Another few yards and he'd be on us!

I stumbled, fell to my knees, jerking Kristen backward.

"Get up!" she shrieked in panic, her eyes wild. "Run, Matt, run!"

She yanked at my arm, pulling me to my feet. She pointed up ahead as we continued to run.

"Right behind those trees!" she cried. "We'll stop him there!"

Her hair had been caught up in a scrunchie, but had come free. It tumbled over her face and shoulders. The only thing I could see in the moonlight were her eyes—round, wide, yet glinting with determination. The Fearless Wonder wasn't about to be beaten by a common werewolf. *I'll never make fun of my cousin again*, I swore at that moment, even as Cherkas (now the Hairy Horror) snapped at our heels.

Raging and snarling, it bounded directly to my right.

I lifted the Super Soaker and shot it blindly at the creature.

Most of the stream fell harmlessly away from the body, but a faint spray caught its tail. The werewolf yelped in pain and fell back.

"Up ahead," Kristen said in a frantic whisper, as we rounded a bend. "We'll be safe."

I glanced over my shoulder. The werewolf had gotten to its feet and was coming after us with renewed fury.

We slipped and slided our way down a grassy slope that led to a stream.

"He can't cross water," Kristen shouted. "Once we get to the other side we'll be all right."

As if reading our minds, the Horror put on extra speed. With a long, rage-filled howl that made my skin crawl, it launched itself down the slope and charged.

Kristen was already splashing halfway through the stream. I was closer to the bank when the huge furry paw swiped out and caught me. I was dragged back to the grass. Shouting for help, I stared up at the great snout, the fangs that were opened, dripping in anticipation. A horrible sound rumbled from deep in the animal's throat.

"Kristen!" I screamed, wrestling with the werewolf, kicking out in panic and desperation.

The pointed yellow fangs came closer.

Just before the tips reached my exposed neck, I saw Kristen hurl something at the animal.

"Now you must be destroyed!" she shouted.

The object hit the werewolf squarely on its snout and fell to the ground.

The werewolf stiffened with a cry, immediately releasing me. I dropped to the grass and rolled away, terrified it would come after me again.

But the Hairy Horror was in too great agony to pursue me. It howled in pain and shock, rising to its hind legs. It rose and rose until it stood taller than any man I'd ever met, baring its teeth in an awful, cheated snarl. Blood streamed from the wound on its snout, hissing and flowing like lava from a volcano. It trailed down the were-wolf's fur, making a phosphorescent pool around its legs.

And all the while it swayed and howled, turning its furnace-red eyes up toward the full moon. The eyes turned back to me and I stared in horrified fascination as the orangey flames inside the pupils slowly died to charred, black holes. The werewolf swiped out blindly, then shuddered and toppled to the ground like a fallen tree. It bounced with the impact, then rolled down the slope into the stream.

The water hissed and sizzled as if touching a live wire. Something flashed below the surface. There was the hot smell of something burning, and then a vapor rose from the stream. Kristen hurriedly skirted the area where the werewolf had been—killed? vaporized?—and joined me on the bank. Together we peered into the water, but there was nothing to be found. The Hairy Horror had been destroyed.

My cousin and I stared at each other and drew a deep, shuddery breath of relief.

"Did he bite or scratch you?" Kristen asked.

Examining myself with trembling fingers, I let out a shaky laugh. "No scratches or nibbles. All those extra layers came in handy."

"So did this," Kristen said, reaching down and grasping a large object. "This is what saved you."

"My mom's good silver candlestick!" I exclaimed. "How did you think to bring this along?"

"There were a lot of things about Victor Cherkas that didn't make sense," she said. "Remember when he handed me the cutout today and our hands met? He reacted like I burned him. Later on I realized I was wearing my silver bracelet. And when that Doberman came rushing up to us on the dock this morning, he was trying to get at the legs of Victor Cherkas, not the cardboard cutout. The dog sniffed out the presence of the *real* werewolf."

I stared at her with wide eyes. "Yeah, and that's why the cutout ended up in his room at the inn. When he went back to human form, the spirit of the Hairy Horror returned to its place in the picture." I knocked a fist against the side of my head and groaned. "How could I have been so stupid? The signs were there, but I missed them all."

Kristen flicked her long hair back. "I wasn't positive, either. But I had enough suspicions to pack the squirt gun and silver candlestick."

"Thank goodness for your sneaky, suspicious mind," I agreed fervently. "If it hadn't been for you, I would have been covered in fur right about now and sprouting three-inch fangs!"

My cousin's lips twitched into the gloating smirk I used to hate, but now I smiled back gratefully. No doubt about it. The Fearless Wonder had saved the day—and my life.

Without warning, something crashed through the woods.

Instinctively I inched closer to Kristen, until I heard Sean's voice.

"Matt! Kristen!" he shouted. "Where are you guys?"

"Over here by the stream," Kristen yelled.

Sean broke through the thick cluster of trees and stumbled down the slope to join us. He was panting, face scrunched in worry.

"I thought I heard barking or growling coming from over here," he cried, skidding to a stop by the stream. "I thought the werewolf had gotten you!"

"We're fine," I assured him. "The werewolf never had a chance against Kristen and me."

"He's gone," Kristen added, pointing at the water. "Gone for good."

Sean's face crumpled. He shook his head in disbelief.

"You mean I missed all the excitement again?" he moaned. "I'm never going to see the werewolf?"

"Sorry," I said with a happy grin. "I guess a hairy situation wasn't mentioned in your horoscope today!"

Thanksgiving turned out to be fun.

All of my relatives came over for dinner and told my mom what a great meal she had cooked.

It was the party afterward that I cared about. Kristen was celebrating her thirteenth birthday and I had helped my mom secretly bake a big cake late the night before. I hadn't had time to buy my cousin anything, but I handed her a small scroll tied with ribbon when she was opening gifts.

"What's this?" she said, eyeing me suspiciously.

"Open it and see," I retorted.

Kristen muttered, but tore off the ribbon and unrolled the piece of paper.

"It's a gift certificate," I proudly announced. "Good for two tickets to the Palace Theater's matinee tomorrow afternoon."

"What's the movie?" my dad asked, peering over her shoulder.

Kristen looked up at me with a private smile.

"The best werewolf film of all time," she said. *"The Night of the Hairy Horror!"*

"Werewolves again," my mom groaned, throwing her hands up.

"There are no such things as werewolves," Chase piped up. "That's dumb."

"Not in Friendly Corners," I agreed happily, and let out the biggest, most ferocious howl possible.